MW01222168

Sellswords:
Book 1 of The Red Death Series

Copyright 2018 Sandy Addison
Cover Illustration by Anson
Published by Sandy Addison at Smashwords

Acknowledgements

I'd like to thank the following people.

To Matt G: for giving me that confidence so many years ago to actually start down the road that got me here.

To Matt O: for being my longest lasting test reader. His feedback has been invaluable.

To Cliff A: my newest and currently most enthusiastic test reader

To Anson: for allowing me to use the image he created as my cover. If you like his work then I'd highly suggest taking a look at his other pieces at http://anson7.deviantart.com.

And a special thank you to: Bromwen F who insisted that I include shoe descriptions for Sasha and Miri as the got ready for dinner; because 'every woman will want to know what kind of shoes goes with those dresses'

Finally, and a no less important a thank you to Gary Gygax and Dave Anderson; for creating a game that made me want to read; and then want to tell stories.

Dedication

This book is dedicated to my mother. Hey mom when you were quizzing spelling words to me in Grade 5 did you think you'd be reading this?

Table of Contents

Crossroads

The year that I was born the world started to die.

Twenty years ago, the first appearance of the Red Death was recorded by a ranger tracking the Broken Fang tribe of Orcs, and twenty years ago, I was born. I'd like to think that both events were momentous, one that the bards would sing about for ages. Sadly, only the Red Death will be recorded in song: there just aren't enough bards around to compose any songs about lone heroes anymore.

Mind you there aren't enough of anyone now a days. The Red Death took half the population in the five years it took to sweep the land. The Madness did even worst damage over the next ten. Mortal beings have only been able to consider a future in the past few years.

Of course, there are a lot of things out there that makes thinking about that future difficult for most mortals. Cults, demonic and otherwise, Titan Spawn packs, wild undead, the Phoenix Republic, and just plain old fashion bandit/refugee bands. It's enough to keep anyone's gaze on the track just ahead of them and not bother with where the track is actually going.

But some people *are* looking at where the track they're on is going; and it's those people that hire me and my partner.

Why us? Well to answer that some introductions are needed. My name is Sasha Storm Crow. Six years ago, I was struck by lightning in the middle of the largest storm that had been seen around my village for decades. I survived the hit and along with a set of really cool looking lightning scars running across my body the bolt unlocked my latent magical ability and I became what in the old world was termed a 'Storm Powered' wild magic mage. Since then, with the help of Riley and various other arcane types I've not only been able to control my magical powers but grown them as well.

My partner, in more ways than one, goes by Miri. Officially she's an Elf who rather than being a 'longbow airy-fairy' type of Elf, is an 'in your face' melee fighter with a longsword that's as big as she is. Many question how such a petite 'Elf maid' could pick up such a big weapon let alone wield it in combat. Those questions usually end when she takes the head of a rampaging zombie with one swipe or splits a skeleton in two like so much cord wood.

Together we help smaller communities 'handle' some of their problems. Weather that's boosting a town's local militia as they clear out an 'abandoned' manor house, acting as caravan guards for the first merchants going through the hills after spring thaw, or dealing with a Titan Spawn scouting pack before it tells the tribe that's there's easy picking this way.

So far, these jobs have kept us in enough coin to keep us mostly fed with a warm place to stay between jobs. We always have to keep moving though. We're women of prime breeding age; and sooner or later, in every village or town we deal with, someone gets it in their heads that we should be spitting out babies, whether we like the idea or not. Now both Miri and I can dissuade such people from acting on that idea but usually not without knocking a few heads together and occasionally leaving a body in the street.

Which is how we ended up heading west on an Old Imperial Highway in the twilight of a late Fall day; low on food, coin and most importantly luck.

Today that bad luck translated into a steady downpour of cold rain. The magic that kept the Highway in good repair still held, so the flat surface stones were intact and clear of dirt and grass. Unfortunately, the spell that allowed this to happen had been designed and cast in a dry climate. So, under the heavy rain the paved road became so slick that our horses were having difficulty keeping their feet. Our only recourse was to dismount and lead them. Fortunately, Riley loved the rain so he was flying above us, his eyes sharp for trouble. So, when my raven familiar landed on my shoulder I knew I wasn't going to like what he was going to say.

"Crossroads coming up and it looks like they're executing someone," said Riley.

Well that wasn't as bad, for us at least, as it could have been.

"Think we should bypass the situation?" asked Miri.

Looking over the side of the road towards the rain-soaked brush that had once been productive farmland I shivered and said "We'd have to blaze a trail, and get even more soaked. Let's stay on the road. At worst, they'll ask us to bear witness," I replied.

Miri nodded in agreement and we continued our walk in the rain, huddled in our great coats, our hair stuffed under beaver felt tricorne hats. As a Wild Storm Mage, people expect me to love bad weather like this; and while it's true that I have some resistance to the elements, cold isn't one of them. I love warm summer rains or intense lightning storms: Not ice-cold rainfalls with oppressive dark grey clouds with no hope what so ever for lightning. And yes, our hats. coats and boots were enchanted to wick off the wet, but in this kind of weather it hardly mattered; the wet and cold still got through.

The close heavy air and constant patter of rain on stone also damped any sounds around us. So, when the crossroads came into sight neither of us was prepared for what we saw. Whatever town used this crossroads for its executions must have found the need to use it a lot; because there weren't just one gallows but four and each had its own crow picker cage. Two of the cages already had bodies in advance states of decay; while the third's body had animated into something halfway between a zombie and a skeleton.

The fourth crow picker was empty. Its soon to be resident was currently tied naked to its base being flogged.

"It's a woman; she's Fey, our age maybe a bit older. She's still alive but I doubt that she'll be by nightfall," said Miri as we approached.

Damn it; now I was curious. The Fey were related to Elves being taller, more 'civilized' and pompous then their woodland cousins. When the plague hit as a group the Fey had retreated to their home dimension and locked the gates behind them. Whether they'd done so in time to save themselves from the plague or not had caused speculation among the remaining sages for years. Before us, was the answer to that particular question and these idiots were about to kill her.

"You sure she's Fey? I mean it's been twenty years," I said.

Miri gave me a look that she usually gave me when she thought that I was being an idiot, then, despite carrying both a broad bladed short sword and dagger on her belt, Miri walked back to her horse and unslung her longsword. A coming of age gift from her father, the five-foot blade had a flared notched based and ornate hilt that all but screamed pain. It was a magical vicious weapon that seemed to tear wounds wider when Miri got a really solid hit in. With a practised ease, she slung the weapon across her back so that it was in easy reach.

While she did so, I took the time to retrieve Thunder and Lightning from my weather proof pouch of holding on my belt. The daggers had been made for me by one of my Dwarf *uncles*. Thunder was a ten-inch blade of blackened steel that allowed me to better channel and control my magic. Lightning was its twin only made of Silvered steel. Why two blades that basically do the same thing? Well as my uncle said 'you got two hands don't cha'? I've learned never to argue with Dwarf logic. Hanging the two daggers off great coat's belt I nodded to Miri that I was ready, and only then did we continue towards the crossroads.

Along with the young woman being executed there

9

were two hooded executioners and six witnesses. All of whom were dressed in black cloaks and hats. Six officials; shit. While it could be a coincidence, these days the number six tends to be a symbolic number for many of the Cults that have risen since the breaking of the covenant.

They were intent in their business and didn't notice Miri and I until we were less than thirty feet from them. Hearing our horse's hooves on the paving stones, the one who looked our direction nudged his companion who also turned to see who was there. Upon seeing us the second mortal raised his hand: A gesture that caused both of the hooded executioners to stop their flogging. Without even looking to see that they had stopped, he moved towards us raising his hat so that we could better see his face.

He appeared to have an open and honest face whose eyes were filled with blood. This marked him as one of the *Lucky*. He had contracted the Red Death and survived. Few could make such a claim and, in many villages, those that did were considered destined for greatness.

"Greetings strangers: What brings you to this crossroads on such a solemn and wet day?" he asked looking up at the rain-soaked clouds with a rueful smile.

I folded my great coat's collar down showing off my face.

"We're sellswords; between jobs. We're just passing through," I replied cautiously.

"Oh? Our town has need of mercenaries; just take the south fork until you hit the ten-mile mark. There you will find the road that leads to our town. Tell the guard Merlock directed you and he'll take care of you till I return," said the Lucky.

The hairs on the back of my neck rose at this. Why not ask us to wait and comeback with them? Merlock seemed confident enough in his power; he didn't consult with others about making such decisions. What other decisions could he make arbitrarily? I glanced over to Miri and saw the ever so slight adjustment to her shoulder to move her sword from rest to ready. She agreed with me, this situation had just become dangerous.

"We just might do that," I replied my tone as neutral as possible. "So, tell me, what did the prisoner do to warrant her death?"

"Malicious demands her blood and her soul. The safety of the town requires that we deliver on that demand," said Merlock so matter of fact he might as well be talking about the crops.

"Funny how he only wanted my blood after I said 'no' to sharing your bed human," said the Fey through gritted teeth.

Her comment really wasn't appreciated by Merlock whose face lost a bit of that open expression. As if he sensed the man's change of mood, one of the executioners brought his bull whip down hard across the Fey's shoulder blades.

I tried to block her scream from my mind as I asked, again with as neutral a tone as possible, "And who is Malicious?"

"He is the one who has kept our town safe from harm these past years. The one to whom we have re-forged a covenant with. I am his voice within the town and the one who sees that his will is done," said Merlock. His voice getting higher and more tinged with madness as he spoke.

Right it was a demon cult...Miri and I were so not going down to this town. But, just as importantly, we were not going to leave the Fey to them.

"Okay Voice of a Demon, my friend and I aren't really interested in working with the truly insane, so we're going to take the West fork and try to get as much space between you and your town as possible. However, before we leave were going to take the girl with us. Whatever, she's done she sure as the Nine Hells doesn't deserve what you've done to her.

11

Merlock didn't like my answer but neither he nor his companions had a chance to react.

With speed that defied a mortal's reaction, Miri seemed to 'appear' next to the Demon's Voice her longsword not only drawn, which given that had been sheathed on her back was something magical by itself, but its too sharp edge now resting against Merlock's neck.

"Move a muscle and I take your head," she hissed, her fangs had extended and her now red irises looked hungrily at the cult leader.

I wasn't idle as Miri made her move. Grasping Thunder's hilt, I summoned the winds of a tornado and sent them circling around the Fey. While she stayed safe within the eye of the small storm, the two executioners were flung back some twenty feet landing with a soggy thud in the water-logged soil.

I then drew Lightening and let the magical energies run up and down its blade, as I pointed it towards the remaining officials.

"Leave," I said, as I flicked the silver steel blade towards the caged zombie, releasing the magic inside the blade. The lightning bolt arced between the dagger and the monster's head. What little remained of the creature's brains turned instantly to steam and the resulting pressure caused the skull to explode sending bone fragments in a wide circle around the cage.

Saying 'or else' at that time really would have been superfluous.

Looking back and forth between Miri and me, one of the officials squeaked "what sort of demons are you?"

It was Riley who spoke up. "The one with the sword is a Daywalker. While my mistress is a Human Being: A magic wielding, storm manipulating, badass of a Human Being, but a Human Being none the less. I suggest that you follow her instructions and leave."

While the officials were all members of a Demon Cult

they appeared to still possess enough of a sense of self-preservation to actually start to leave. That was until Merlock spoke.

"Fools; once I'm done with the two of you, there won't be enough for a proper sacrifice," he said as his face started to ripple and bloat as he started to change into something else.

What the something else was I'll never know because with a scream of rage Miri spun the longsword away from Merlock in a wide circle that continued as it cut cleanly through the transforming monster's neck from the opposite side. With a spurt of arterial blood that rose some thirty feet into the air; the creature's body fell to the ground before his minions and despite the heavy rain proceeded to burst into flame. The head fell right in front of the remaining five officials with a surprised, almost embarrassed, look upon its partially transformed face.

As if they were a flock of birds the officials, as one, turned and started to run down the southern branch of the crossroads. They were quickly followed by the two executioners.

"Miri see to the Fey. Riley keep an eye on the southern road," I shouted to my companions as I moved back to the horses.

Grabbing the animal's reins, I led them towards the gallows where Miri had dealt with the bindings that kept the Fey restrained with the simple expedience of cutting through them.

Freed the Fey hadn't the strength to keep herself standing and had slid down the gallows to become a shivering heap at its base. Taking a good look at her for the first time, I saw that Miri was right. The Fey 'appeared' to be close to our age, though that could mean that she could have been 20 to 200 years old. My guess was that she was closer to 20. Like many young people in this world her body was covered with a series of garish tattoos and body piercings. One druid I knew said that the harsh body art that many young mortals bore today, was an expression of our inward pain we felt as the world died.

The nipple rings just made me feel like a badass.

Her hair when it was dry was probably the colour of spun gold, but now wet, slicked with her own blood it was shit brown in colour. But her all gold eyes looked up at me defiantly, despite her freezing to death and her back being so much tenderized stake.

Reaching into my horse's saddle bag, I grabbed his extra blanket and moved back to the Fey. Miri took the blanket and wrapped it around the girl. A small whimper of pain passed her blued lips as the coarse wool touched her back.

"Miri, we need to get moving, we need to get out of here, and she needs a warm place if she's going to survive,"

"Which road do we take?" asked Miri.

My partner is far from being stupid, but I am the cleverer of the two of us, so with anything that involves guile she always expects me to come up with the plan.

"North, we need to get as much distance between those cultists and us as possible while we still have some light," I said. "When it's too dark to see, we'll make camp and see about keeping the Fey alive."

My train of thought was interrupted by a sudden burst of evil laughter. Turning around, I was more annoyed than shocked when I realized the laughter was coming from Merlock's head.

"So you're the Storm Crow? I've heard of you, and your Vampire lover. Know that you've taken your last breaths. My master will hunt you down and...," the head's taunt abruptly ended in a scream of pain as Riley ripped out one of its eyes and swallowed it whole.

"What? Still warm eyes are a real delicacy," said the Raven as a way of explanation to the rest of us.

I let of an annoyed sigh and pointed Lightening at the

14

still screaming skull. Riley quickly took flight as I sent several bolts of blazing white energy into the talking head; burning flesh and boiling away grey matter, until like the zombie earlier, the skull exploded into pieces.

Once I was sure it could no longer listen, I turned back to Miri and the Fey. "Right North is screwed for us; they might expect us to take the West road which still might be a good option."

I paused, thinking down several paths all at once. What I finally came up with would be a gamble but it was our best bet, "We'll head back down the East highway again. A couple of miles back, there was the remains of a dirt road heading north. We'll take that road and hope it leads to some sort of shelter," I said to the others.

Miri just nodded in agreement and after quickly cleaning and then sheathing her sword she picked up the Fey as if she'd weighted nothing more than a child.

"I remember that road. Get onto your horse. You'll ride with her while I lead the horses back to the road," she said.

That made sense and as soon as I was in the saddle and had my feet in the stirrups, Miri handed me the Fey, who now safe, decided to start babbling deliriously. I grunted as I pulled her up in front of me and held her side saddle.

"Do you have her?" asked Miri.

"Yes, let's get going," I said. I'm not much bigger than Miri so there was more than enough room for both the Fey and myself, on the saddle.

With that Miri headed back down the eastern highway. She set a brisk pace jogging down the road and forcing the two horses into a fast trot. A mile into the trip my legs were feeling the stress of keeping up and away from the saddle but our delirious new companion didn't seem to mind. Fortunately, soon after I'd started to curse Miri for having me ride a trotting horse, we came upon the remains of the dirt road. Once we were on non-magical dirt track she

15

remounted and pulled the Fey girl onto her horse.

"We're going to leave a pretty clear trail," said Riley as he landed on my shoulder. During our trip back, the rain had stopped but the ground was still waterlogged enough to make it impossible not to turn up mud. As well the sky was still full of clouds, thus darkness would fall far faster and be far deeper than the time of year would dictate. Miri's sharp elf eyes wouldn't be much more use than mine.

"I know but that can't be helped," I replied to the Raven, as we set off on a steady walking speed up the trail. I was gambling that we'd be long gone by the time the townspeople would think of checking this way.

Despite the muddy conditions, we were initially able to make pretty good time. The horses were in good shape having walked unburdened most of the day, and Miri was still able to see through the mist and darkening skies long after things got to the point where I was barely able to see her horse ahead of me.

After an hour, Miri brought up her horse short. "Our luck may have turned Sasha, the fields up ahead looked tilled," she said.

Reaching into my pouch of holding I pulled out a small box with a small door on one side. Opening the door, the glowing red light of a crystal with light spell permanently cast into it was released. The door allowed me to direct the light around me and hopefully didn't give our position away to any hostile creatures of the night.

Looking around it appeared that my friend was correct, there were tilled fields around us, fallow and ready for the first winter snow; a hopeful sign. Two minutes later we were not only riding through cropland but further down the road Miri reported seeing the smoke and embers of cooking fires rising from what looked to be a well-kept cheery village.

"Maybe they keep the road near the highway in poor shape as a defensive measure," said Miri.

16

I stayed silent and sniffed the air. As a wild mage, I lack the formal magical training of a book mage (aka wizard), but I make up for it by being naturally attuned to the patterns and flow of the magical energy around me. And right now, those senses told me that the natural flow of magic was being severely disrupted.

As we came to the village I could tell Miri was also becoming concerned. Unlike most post plague villages, this one had neither a wall nor blockhouse for defence. What was even stranger, was that the entire village appeared to not only be awake but in the village common. However, their attention was not on the three water logged strangers; instead they were all concentrated on the village well. As we looked on the village men were hauling on the bucket rope pulling up what appeared to be a great weight. Their efforts were rewarded by the head and shoulders of a teenage human male coming into view, in his arms was a young human girl and she held on tightly to what appeared to be a stuffed clothed rabbit. All of this was clearly visible under the warm glowing light from the village priest's upraised staff. Seeing the priest, I realized why the lack of defences, while there was some danger, if we played this right we could use this situation to our advantage.

As soon as they came into view there were cries of joy and both children were wrapped in dry blankets and taken indoors, but not before the boy gave a couple of other male youths a hard stare that made them both flinch. Children rescued, the rest of the villagers started to return their homes, it was only then that a few noticed us standing on the edge of the light.

There were a few startled cries and a couple of the older men grabbed up handy clubs, while others disappeared into the gloom, no doubt to retrieve weapons. But the priest had a different reaction. Boldly he walked towards us, so that we were brought further into the light of his glowing staff.

"Hello strangers. What brings you to our humble village so late at night?" he asked. Like Merlock before, he had an open and honest face. His religious robes were obvious made from local cloth; sturdy and lacking any finery.

However, the fact that he was a priest caused Miri to unconsciously move her hand towards her weapon's hilt.

"We're looking for a warm dry place to stay, your holiness. We found a fellow traveller beaten and robbed on the road and I fear for her life without proper shelter.

The priest's face became concerned when he saw the blanket rapped Fey. "Merciful Gods, of course of course, bring her into my home I have a warm fire already ablaze. It's late but I'm sure I can get some warm food for all three of you."

One of the men moved towards Miri to take the Fey and my partner looked towards me with a look of confusion.

"Let the man help Miri," I said, then turning back towards the priest I said "We have our own supplies, holiness there is no need for you to raid your winter stores for us; but if we can stable our horses that would be of great assistance."

"Why of course, my house has a stable for visiting clergy, please come with me. Oh, I'm Benedict by the way, and welcome to the village of One Spot," said the cleric.

"I am Sasha and this is Miri. Before we stable our horses, I'd like to see to our unfortunate companion," Glancing over to the well I said, "Looks as if you had some excitement tonight as well."

The cleric smiled embarrassingly "A game of keep away gone too far. Sarah loves that rabbit like a mother loves a newborn. Mathew and Gregory didn't expect her to lunge for it when they threatened to drop it into the well. Both she and the rabbit went over the side. Thank goodness Samuel had the courage to follow her in and keep her head above the water, but I'd expect nothing less from the headman's son," said Benedict with obvious pride.

"Lucky, he was there," I agreed.

"Oh, yes but such energy is expected after a winter of idleness. The children will all be tired enough once the planting starts," said the cleric sagely, as we moved toward a well-built stone house next to a much larger building.

Miri paused by both horses to grab our saddlebags. Moving quickly, she fell in step with me and with a whisper asked "Sasha what are you doing? This place is all wrong, there's no way it safe here."

"There's some danger yes, but I know what we're dealing with and it's the best chance the Fey has of living, and I have a feeling that no cultist would step foot in this village," I replied.

One of the great strengths of our partnership is the trust we put in each other. Miri trusted that I knew what I was doing, and I hoped that that trust wasn't misplaced.

We entered the cleric's home and it appeared to be a warm and welcoming place of several rooms built around a central fireplace. The entrance opened into a large living area, which appeared to be used for both eating and company, it was filled with simple yet well-built furniture, including rugs on the stone floor and a table covered with parchment, ink wells, and several candles.

"My apologies; you caught me amid my monthly correspondence," said Benedict as he tried to clean pens close inkwell and roll up paper all at the same time.

"The bedrooms to the right," he said indicating the right-hand door.

"Thank you, Benedict, but I'm afraid that our friend is going to be in need of a more direct heating source," I replied.

"Could you put our friend on that rug next to the fire?" I asked the man carrying the Fey.

He complied with a little grunt.

"Thank you for your help, now if you'll excuse me were going to need the room," I said to the men in my most dismissive voice. I then started to remove horse blanket from the Fey, showing far too flesh to be 'proper'.

"Ah. Yes, well we'll get your mounts into the stable," said Benedict pulling the other man out of the room.

Alone I turned to Miri and said "There's little that you can do to rewarm her, why don't you see to the horses. Comb them out and dry them as best you can. Give them all of our remaining oats, but don't let them eat anything from the village. Once they're settled put all of their blankets over them, they'll be dry but cold tonight." As I talked I handed her the horse blanket that had been wrapping the Fey.

Miri just nodded, not fully understanding what was going on, but trusting that I knew what I talking about. She did however; loosen the Imperial short sword on her belt before leaving the house.

"Miri," I called out to my partner just before she left for the stables. "Be polite to any of the villagers you talk to, and that goes double for Benedict."

My partner gave me a look that was best described as 'yes mother' and left into the night.

Alone with the Fey I quickly wrapped her in my own bedroll, in front of the cheery fire in the hearth. The heat felt good on my skin and I had to slow my movement so that I didn't break out in a sweat. Slowly I fed her one of our precious healing potions, and her colour started to improve as the welts and cuts on her back quickly healed leaving unscarred flesh in their place.

As great a lifesaving aid as healing potions are, they can't heal exposure. Turning away from the fire, I hung up my outer clothing to dry and I stripped down to my undergarments before I joined the Fey in my bedroll so that I could warm her with my own body heat. I moved quickly before the chill of the home soaked into my body.

20

"This is very clever Sasha, and I think it will save the Fey's life. I'm pretty sure she wouldn't have survived in the open," Riley said to me as he settled in for the night among the rafters. "To bad Miri wasn't able to feed on any of those bastards. She's too cold to take over for you."

I nodded in both agreement and understanding. This was going to be an uncomfortable night for me but that couldn't be helped. You see while Miri *appears* to be fully Elven, she's actually half vampire, a Daywalker in today's slang. Her father was *once* an Elf but at some point, in his life he was turned into a vampire. The necrotic magic that keeps a full vampire 'alive' is sometimes strong enough to keep them fertile. So, when they mate, beings like Miri can result. A still mortal being; that possesses, to a lesser degree, the powers and hindrances of their undead parent. So, for example, Miri doesn't need blood to live. However, without it her body grows cold and her complexion pales to the point of being translucent.

After an hour, the door opened and Miri re-entered Benedict's home our saddles and tack in both hands and her longsword once again on her back. "The horses are settled in," she said as she stripped out of her wet outer clothing. Moving towards the fire she warmed her hands and then opened her own pouch of holding and pulled out her bedroll. Stripping out of her own clothing she turned and looked surprised at the fire. She moved back and forth from the fire to the door before Riley sighed and said, "just accept it for now. Wrap yourself in that chair over there and keep your sword handy."

Miri muttered something about lower intelligent fowl and then did what my familiar suggested. "Is she going to make it?" she asked once she was settled in.

"If a Fey's body operates like other mortals yes she should be fine. I got a healing potion into her for the physical damage and I can feel her body warming," I replied.

21

"I hope she's bloody worth it," said Miri a note of frustration.

"Giving a damn can be a bitch sometimes," I agreed as I wrapped my arms around the girl and settled in for the night.

**

Dawn broke far too soon as far as I was concerned, but there was no sound of rain, so that was something. As soon as my memory came back to what happened yesterday, I checked the Fey and found that she was sleeping soundly her body warm. Her dry hair looked to be a tangled mess, but I had guessed right; dry it was a golden blonde in colour.

As I slowly disentangled myself from both her and the blankets I slowly got up into the cold room and got dressed in some dry work clothing. Despite my best efforts at being quiet, Miri had awoken as soon as I had started to stir.

"Sleep well?" I whispered to my partner.

"Surprisingly well, given where we are," she replied. Daywalkers actually do need to sleep, just not as long as other mortals. Miri then got up and twisted her back hard enough that several bone breaking cracks filled the room. With a satisfied sigh, she also proceeded to sort through her things to find some new clothing.

I've often thought that the sound of Miri cracking her back could wake the dead, and I had some proof of this fact when the Fey moaned and twisted around see where the sound came from.

"Hello?" she said hesitancy as she sat up and look upon Miri and myself.

"Good morning, you're looking a lot better. I'm Sasha this is Miri and the poor excuse for a feather duster is Riley," I said as cheerfully as possible.

"Sariel, nice to meet you, and thanks for saving my life yessssterday?" replied the Fey not sure of how long she'd been incoherent. She stretched and only then did she realize

22

that she was still completely naked under the bedding and covered herself.

"I know were not your size, but I'm sure we can cobble something together that would work," I said to Sariel reassuringly.

"No need," she replied as she made a cutting jester with her left hand. Magic energies were shifting through the room like a small vortex, as her hand seemed to disappear into thin air only to come back a second later with a large sack. It was then that I noticed that her arm tattoo not only had ink but several embedded gems worked into it, and they all glowed brightly as arcane energy coursed through them.

Riley let out a long whistle, which given that he didn't have lips has always been a bit disconcerting to me, and said "Embedded magic; well that's something new. Sasha, I think we have our next research project."

"Later Riley we still have work to do here," I said, though I had to agree I really wanted to know what other tricks Sariel had.

"Work?" asked the Fey as she pulled a complete change of clothing including a large warm looking cloak from the sack.

"Yes, we need to put things right in this village; it's the least we can do to help, given that we were able to take advantage of this place last night to keep both you and us alive," I replied.

By the time I was able to throw on my own clothing and pull my hair back Sariel was dressed as well. Though she appeared fine, and the healing potion had left her skin clear; the effort of getting dressed appeared to tire her. A reminder of just how close she'd come yesterday to death.

Once we were all dressed, I opened the door on what at least was starting to be a nice day. The clouds were breaking up providing a lovely orange dawn. Around us the village was getting up and men and women of all ages were getting started their morning chores. I saw the young girl Sarah walk by carrying her now dried rabbit tightly in her arms. She saw me and gave me a big smile and waved hello. In the middle of all this daily chaos stood Benedict in the exact same spot that he had been when we first saw him last night.

"Good morning! Your companion seemed much improved from last night," he said his face in a big grin.

"Yes, she is, my thanks for your help," I started.

"She still looks a bit pale; perhaps you three should stay for the day? I could have breakfast brought to you," he said as a note of desperation crept into his voice.

Oh, how I so wanted to somewhere else, I hesitated for a second an excuse already forming onto my lips, but then I felt Riley's claws dig a bit into my shoulder.

"You know what has to be done," he said quietly into my ear.

"Many thanks Benedict and we might stay but it's time for you to go," I started, "It okay you can move on, my friends and I will give everyone a decent burial and we will remember you and your village and how you helped keep us alive,"

The Priest expression became a mixture of confusion warring with pain, but he remained silent.

"You're dead Benedict, you and your village have been dead for close to twenty years. The Blood Plague took you all and it was so quick your soul couldn't believe it; you didn't want to believe and finally you chose a different path.

"No, no: No! They were my friends my family I help bring many of them into this world, I married them, blessed their children, but when they needed me most…"

Around us the village started to change, first the people started to disappear, then the animals and finally the carefully maintained huts started to collapse.

"There was nothing you could have done, no cleric, no

24

druid, no wizard no king could cure the plague everyone was helpless before it. Their deaths weren't your fault," I half lied. This had been a good man; he didn't need to hear the full truth of who was responsible.

"Really?" he asked.

"Really, Benedict. As I said go in peace we'll make sure that everyone is taken care of," I said to him again.

Benedict sighed as if a heavy weight had been lifted off of his shoulders. "Make sure you bury Sarah with her rabbit, she'd be lost without it," he said with a final large smile. Then the ghost of the holy man disappeared like the morning mist.

The child and that damn rabbit. That must have been a proud moment for him; the village gathering as one to save the life of their smallest. No wonder as a ghost he had relived the event again and again. He must have been a powerful presence in the village. Certainly, his spirit was strong enough to recreate it and the surrounding land to near perfection. The fires giving off heat only when you paid attention to them; was the only mistake. Well that and his own fixation about it being spring.

Such hauntings are not uncommon these days, and while this one had been benevolent, not all are. That's why it's best not to eat anything, accepting too much of a ghost's hospitality can bind you into the illusion and you can end up as trapped as the ghosts.

Just another hazard of the road in these strange and chaotic times. But we were safe for now. Benedict's ghost had, in his unwillingness to let go of life, managed to save the life of another. Reaching into my pouch I pulled out a small Dwarven crafted shovel and tossed it to Miri.

"Miri, you start digging the grave, Sariel and I will get the bodies that Riley spots," I said to everyone.

Time to repay the debt.

25

Fairy Godsister

Chapter One

"So that is the Great Green? It doesn't really look all that impressive from here," said Sariel looking out at the city's harbour.

"That's because this is a small arm of the sea. Thirty kilometers east it widens into a sea so wide you can't see the other side from the highest mountain," I replied a bit testy. Sariel had been journeying with us for two weeks; and while she was pleasant enough company her 'nothing here compares to the Fey Reich' attitude was starting to get on my nerves.

"I'm sure it's quite impressive," Sariel replied trying not to sound patronizing, but failing miserably. "But shouldn't we worry about paying for the accommodations before Miri gets back from stabling the horses?"

The Fey had a point. We'd had to make a major detour around the region controlled by the followers of Misery which had resulted in a far harder and longer trip than either Miri or I had expected. Sariel had been the cause of that detour. She was a native of the Fey Reich; one of the three dimensions that made up the Inner Realm. It had cut all ties with the Mid and Shadow Reichs when the Red Death had hit. Nothing had been heard from its inhabitants in twenty years.

Then Sariel had been travelling through the centre of the Demon Cult's domain. Taller, more regal cousins, of the Imperium Elves, the Fey had unfortunately caught the eye of one of Misery's disciples. When she spurned his advances, the disciple had Sariel seized and condemned to public torture and execution.

That was where Miri, Riley and I had stepped in and rescued our Fey damsel in distress.

Fortunately, this damsel in distress had actually come with her own supplies, which she'd been more than willing to add to our meager provisions. So at least we'd not spent the last few days hungry.

But finally, we'd made; to our third choice of southern cities: The City of Florenz. Once, and still is by its resident's, it had been called the 'Jewel of the Great Green'. But now titles like 'Great Green's Swamp' or 'Imperium's Cesspool' are used. Florenz had once been one of the major entry ways for trade and people to the Imperium. It had been said that the streets had been paved in gold and that a person with ambition and a head for business could start the day a popper and end it with the wealth of kings.

That had of course been before it had been the entryway for the Red Death into the Imperium itself. Despite warnings, people hadn't been ready. They'd taken comfort in their public health measures and the assurance of the clerics and the book mages that they could divine when the plague would hit and cure all those inflicted before the outbreak could spread. They'd done it before with similar illnesses and they'd would do it again with this so call Plague. They were wrong. The Red Death came upon Florenz like a lightning bolt out of a clear blue sky. The clerics of the God of Cities and the Sun (curse their names to the abyss) said that they had tried to cure those inflicted but their prayers did not help. In a desperate move, they had let the first victims die and then tried to return them to life.

They failed yet again, and that was when the panic had started. Nine out of ten citizens had died or fled the city spreading both the plague and the tales of the Gods first breach of The Compact between the Gods and the mortals The Three Reichs. Within a year many of the surviving citizens of Florenz had returned; accept that is for the nobles who had run the city.

Into this leadership vacuum stepped the guilds: merchants and craftsmen these men and women of all races started to rebuild. The most successful (or ruthless depending upon who you ask) guild unfortunately was the Thieves and Smugglers Union. It wasn't long before they'd cowed the others and opened the ports to pirates and smugglers. Now a large part of Florenz's wealth came from refitting pirate ships and fencing their ill-gotten gains throughout the Imperium. Such a large network of illegal trade meant that sellswords who kept to a contract, and keep their mouths shut; were in high demand. This was why Miri and I decided to make for Florenz for our winter billeting: we needed the money. We'd not backed any winning sides during the summer campaigning and caravan season (not to mention rescuing Fey maidens from the gibbet) so we had just enough coin to get us here.

Turning back to Sariel I asked "You still willing to pay for a room? Miri and I can pay you back once we get our advance."

The Fey nodded her head in acknowledgement "I'm willing to go a week, after will depend on what the job situation looks like. I'm grateful for saving my life, but that doesn't mean I trust you when it comes to money," she said.

"That's more than fair," I replied. Old timers might have been offended by an offer of just a week's lodging for a life, but The Plague had made life a lot cheaper.

As we walked to Miri's preferred Inn, Riley landed on my shoulder. "I didn't see anyone in town that wants us dead. Though there are some Elven Breed Hunters along the docks that Miri should avoid," he said as I scratched him under the chin. The Raven always liked to fly over a town we were in to check it out. We didn't have many enemies that outright wanted to kill us but we did have some.

"Anyone take a potshot at you this time?" I teased.

"No; they must have had a good harvest this year," he replied sourly.

As we approached the Inn Riley croaked quietly in my ear "any bets on the reaction that everyone is going to give the throwback?"

I smiled and shook my head no; but it was a good question. It appeared that during the twenty or so years of separation between us and the Fey, that fashions had gone in different directions. Sariel's tunic with the extra-large sleeves, multi coloured patched hose, turned down black leather boots, and her cloak made her look like an actress from a period drama that were so popular now. Both Miri and I had tried to tell her that she looked ridiculous but she insisted that she'd done her research and this was the 'cutting edge of adventurer chic.'

Yeah, I didn't understand it either. Oh well she'd get the idea soon enough.

The Taleless Rat was one of several Inns and Taverns that catered to the mercenary/sellsword elements within the city. I liked it because the beds were free of bugs and the food was worth the price that you paid. Miri liked it because the owners respected their customers' privacy and expected everyone to do the same. So, when Sariel, Riley and I came in, the Fey was underwhelmed by the response we got. A few of the patrons looked up, saw that we didn't pose a threat and then returned to whatever beverage they were drinking. We did get the usual appraisals and leers that are part in parcel of young women entering a drinking establishment but that was as far as it went. My female sellsword predecessors had long ago made it clear to anyone who was stupid enough to give them unwanted attention, the big error of their ways.

"Winter Queen! You can practically hear the magic hum in this room," Sariel said as she looking around. Finally; the Fey was impressed by *something*.

Inside the Inn were two dozen mercenaries of all sorts. Mages of all three varieties sat down with both heavily armoured monster hunters and lightly equipped musketeers.

Against the wall were storage racks holding muskets, two handed swords, war bows, and more varieties of polearms than had any right to exist. Humans were in the majority but there were more than a few Dwarves and male Elves scattered among the crowd. There were even four Hobgoblins from the eastern lands in the mix.

"Impressive isn't it; and the truly ironic thing is that most of them are completely clueless," said Riley.

Sariel turned to the Raven and said "but how can they…not know?"

They've no understanding of the world before them: this is their normal. My guess is that a higher proportion of them survived the plague; there is a higher predisposition for luck in their lives after all. And you know what is really scary; their total number actually increased after the plague," replied my familiar.

"Also, we usually have more important things to worry about then the total number of magic wielders and hero types in the world," I said a bit annoyed by the conversation. The number of times that I'd fallen to sleep while the Birdbrain had prattled on about the changes in magic was embarrassing. I got the Raven to hop on my hand and moved him over to Sariel's shoulder.

"Make yourselves useful while you talk. Get a table as near the fire as you can, while I secure us a room and something to eat," I said to the both of them.

"Will they have coffee here?" asked the Fey, her face full of hope.

"They should, I'll get a carafe if they do," I replied I then turned to head up to the bar, but then turned remembering something important. "One more thing, leave the chair closest to the fire open, Miri needs the extra heat."

"Yes mother," replied Riley, before returning to his conversation with our newest companion.

Getting back to business I weaved my way through the random assortment of tables towards the bar and a familiar face.

"Sasha! I thought that was you, but your partner sure as the Nine Hells wasn't Miri," said Samuel. The old barman must have been pushing fifty, yet he moved with the energy of a much younger man. As far as I knew he'd been the owner/barman of *The Taleless Rat* his entire life. The place was home and his customers were his family even if we were just there for the night.

"Samuel, we stayed here two days a year ago; how do you remember my name?" taken aback, but secretly very pleased, by his friendly greeting.

"Two attractive young women, one silver haired with a *very* talkative raven on her shoulder and the other a blood red haired elf who decked two bullies, twice her size, that were trying to get under my daughter's skirts. Just lucky I guess," he replied with a smile so genuine that it was worth the entire trip just to see it. "What can I get you?"

"Your cleanest room for a week, use of the bathhouse later today to start with, and right now, whatever you had on for lunch for three and a fresh carafe of coffee. And before you ask: yes, were willing to wait for the pot to be brewed," I replied as a past over several hardly clipped silver pieces.

"Ah it's such a pleasure to deal with a knowledgeable customer," said Samuel as he took the silver.

Smiling a thank you, I returned back to where Riley and Sariel were sitting having an animated discussion, which quieted as I sat down beside them.

"So, what are we having?" asked Sariel. She always seemed to be interested in what we were going to be eating.

"I'm guessing, but most likely the last of the fresh bread, cheese and the first of the year's pickled vegetables, along freshly made coffee. I also got their cleanest room for a week and use of the bathhouse for the evening," I replied.

"A bath's an excellent notion we could all use one, I believe. Is it acceptable to also wash our undergarments in the bath as well, or do they have pay separate for that service?" she asked.

"If you're just washing a couple of shifts there shouldn't be a problem, but if you're looking at doing more, then yeah you should talk to Samuel about that," I replied.

The Fey nodded satisfied with the answer. Looking up she then said "Ah it appears you were very correct about the composition of our lunch though, I'm not sure of the amount."

With that, Liza, one of Samuel's daughters, came forward with a trey heaped with food. Two loaves of northern rye, along with a pot of butter or a runny cheese, I wasn't sure which yet, and a large bowl of pickled vegetables, and much to my surprise two halves of cold roast chicken.

"Your coffee will be here shortly Sasha," Liza said as she presented everything to us. She was a curvy girl whose quick smile and twinkling eye meant that she rarely lacked for attention.

"Please let Miri know that if she needs *anything* else she should let me know," she continued, her voice turning husky with desire and her eyes widening in anticipation.

Inwardly I sighed but said *without* the least bit of jealousy in my voice "I'll be sure to let her know."

Liza gave me another brilliant smile and turned her attention back to other customers within the bar.

"She's rather brazen," said Sariel as she forked a helping of vegetables onto her plate.

"It's not what you think. Last time she was here Miri was hungry and made the mistake of feeding on her. The girl found the entire experience a bit too 'enjoyable' and is desperate for another experience. Miri despite looking physically like an Elf is in fact a Daywalker. The child of a Vampire and a mortal, Daywalkers possess some of the power of their Vampire parent, increased speed and strength for example, but few of the weaknesses. While a Daywalker doesn't need to feed on mortal blood to survive for example they should do so as part of a balanced diet. Like Humans should eat green vegetables or Dwarves drink beer with lots of hops for example.

Sariel's expression made it clear that she thought that I was joking, but when I didn't give a punch line she just said quietly "you're serious."

"I blame all the bards singing songs and telling stories about tragic vampire lovers, it's warped the minds of today's youth," I replied.

"She's close to your age. Doesn't mean you've been warped as well?" countered the Fey.

"I'm her lover. We discovered a long time ago that sharing a bed and sharing blood *do not* mix. As her significant other, I might get a little protective of Miri when it comes to who she eats but I think that's pretty reasonable," I said with maybe a bit more honesty than I intended.

"For the record when Sasha says 'protective' translate that to jealous and you're closer to the truth," commented Riley as he stole a pickled onion from Sariel's plate.

"You know Riley, they *will* cook any wild game that a patron brings in here," I said smiling broadly.

The raven appeared to be unconcerned by my threat; though he did hop over to the Fey's side of the table before stealing a large piece of bread from her plate.

"What did the feather duster say this time?" asked Miri as she moved past our table to hang up her longsword along with the other weapons. Coming back, I noticed that she really did need to feed. The blood vessels under her skin were clearly visible in her cheeks and she moved with a listlessness that was caused by far more than just a lack of sleep.

As soon as she sat down, Riley leaped onto Miri shoulder and squawked, "Sasha's being mean to me!"

Miri sighed but didn't bat an eye when she said "Sasha stop threatening to hurt your familiar. That's my job."

"Yeah that's her…wait what?" Riley managed to say before as Miri grabbed the Raven around his legs and threw him back towards me. I caught the mass of black feathers.

Sariel looked shocked at everything that was happening and the look upon her face was enough to send Miri, Riley and myself in uncontrollable laughter.

"It's an old routine we do. It's all an act," Riley explained.

"It's mostly an act," Miri said as she broke up one of the chicken halves putting the leg and thigh onto her plate.

About that time Liza returned with the fresh coffee. She put down the tray and gave Miri a large wink before she left.

Fresh food, hot coffee, baths, and an actual bed to sleep in; I realized that there was only one thing missing from making this a perfect night.

"Liza mentioned that if there was anything else you needed you had but to ask," I said casually to my Daywalker lover.

"Really?" replied Miri.

Chapter Two

The rain that had dogged our trip south continued the morning of our first full day in Florenz but I didn't give a shit. I'd had a bath, slept in a bed behind a locked door, eaten a meal I hadn't had to cook; and most importantly, Miri and I had managed to grab a good hour of privacy for ourselves while Sariel had used the bathing room to wash both herself and some clothing. Having just fed on Liza, Miri was a randy as a teenage male. That was pretty usual for her after she's fed. Sometimes that can be a pain but last night it had been heaven. Though; I did have to use a magic ritual to 'freshen' up the sheets afterwards.

So, as we all headed to the mustering hall to look for work, Miri and I had that 'I had great sex last night' step. My greatly improved outlook on life didn't stop me from dressing for the weather though. Along with our beaver felt Tricornc hats Miri and I continued to wear our heavy leather great coats that had served us both well over the past few years. Along with being magicked to keep the rain and cold out, both had been reinforced across the chest and in the joints by boiled leather plates that added the extra protection that sellswords needed today to defend against the many monsters (both on two and four legs) that were a hazard of the job. Miri had taken the protection a step further by riveting dozens of metal scales across the shoulders and collar to provide some extra protection she felt she needed from the powerful down strokes from weapons that she often faced due to her being smaller than many of her opponents.

Sariel on the other hand.

Sariel had, once again, dressed to the dictates of her personal sense of 'mercenary' fashion. The bottom layer had started with one of her silk blouses, a blue so bright it almost glowed, with multiple layers of silk along the arms causing the sleeves to puff out three to four times their

37

regular size. Overtop this she wore what appeared to be plates of boiled leather dyed black. From a distance, it looked to be a rich noble's steel half-plate right down to the gold filigree on the otherwise black surface. But what really took the cake for me were the skin tight black leather pants. First, they left nothing to the imagination as to the shape of her lower body, but I had to wonder how she was able to bend over let alone move. Yet she did move; as easy as she was in a pair of light wool hose. Over top of her 'armour' Sariel wore a heavy cloak of black and blue wool that did little to allow the Fey to 'blend in' her surroundings.

"You do not have clothing rituals in the Mid Reich?" was her only response when I asked about her clothing; as if that explained everything.

Of course, all three of us 'accessorized' our looks: translation we were armed to the teeth. We were heading to a sellsword guild hall after all, and showing that you were at least competent enough with your weapons to carry them correctly was the first step in getting work.

I was the lightest armed with just Thunder and Lightning my two stilettos which helped me to better channel my magical powers, belted at my waist. Belted around Sariel's waist were a fighting dagger and one-handed arming sword set that were coloured to be perfect accessories to her armour. And just because they were cool the Fey had a hilt of a throwing dagger protruding from the top of each of her boots. Miri had a similar set of blades around her waist though hers were an original Old Empire short sword and thrusting dagger that had been in her family for centuries. They're clean efficient lines were completely unlike her other family gift, the five-foot longsword that she wore over one shoulder. That weapon had been created by both by design and magic to inflict nasty jagged wounds in an opponent. Miri cleaned and oiled the blade daily and I'd never seen her do so without drawing blood before she'd been done.

38

The muster hall was a blockhouse that had once been part of the city's inner defences. When the Guilds had taken over; the Mercenary Guild had quickly formed, and taken it as its headquarters. Since that time the Mercenary Guild had been *the* place where employers came when they wanted competent and more importantly reliable sellswords in the Southern Imperium.

It wasn't really that much to look at from an aesthetic perspective. It was a large square building with its second story larger than the first. Each of the stories were made of foot thick stone covered with loopholes and arrow slits to allow everything from gunpowder weapons to war bows and spells to be used in the building's defence. Presently only the upper story loopholes could be effectively used though. The lower stories' defences being covered by layers of cheap paper sheets and flower paste so thick that is looked as if the walls had been whitewashed. The sheets were either posted by potential employers announcing contracts or by various mercenary groups themselves advertising for work. I took it as a hopeful sign that many of the sheets were new and there seemed to be a large crowd of sellswords of all race and types around the walls checking the latest posting.

"Sariel how literate are you in low Dwarf?" I asked.

"About as good as that language allows anyone to be considered 'literate'," she replied.

I bristled a bit at her dig at the first language I learned my letters with, but let that pass. "Good: go with Miri and check out the posted jobs. We're looking for garrison or patrol work, not caravans. If you see something that looks promising show it to Miri." I said.

"Alright and where will you be?" she asked.

Before I answered I pulled out a silver steel medallion maybe four centimetres across. It was on a chain of similar metal from my belt pouch of holding. Hanging it from my neck I said, "I'm a member in good standing of The Guild so I'm allowed inside the blockhouse itself."

The Fey looked at me quizzically trying to understand why that was significant.

"Guild officials always have the freshest gossip, and recruiters aren't allowed to post their sheets until they've been stamped by the guild. So, I can peruse the line and get first shot at any jobs before they're posted," I said answering her unspoken question.

Once Sariel understood, she immediately saw the logic and sent me with a shooing motion towards the entrance. I gave her a smile and with Riley on my shoulder ventured inside the building.

I was met with a visible wall of tobacco smoke mixed with the smell of unwashed male bodies, gunpowder, half a dozen mixtures used to water proof oil skin and I don't know how many brands of perfume which were supposed to cover up those other smells.

"I think I'll keep Miri company outside," said Riley as he stuffed his beak behind my ear and deep under my collar.

"Oh no you don't I need you here, besides I know you've dealt with worst," I said.

"I knew that there were eyes in that mix, I just had to find them. Here there's nothing to nibble on," replied my familiar.

"Sasha!" screamed a high, very female, voice from across the room.

With a big smile, I turned and saw Keira of Quellwasser come running towards me a big smile on her face. Before I knew it, I was engulfed in a hug that brought tears to my eyes. Not because of any great physical strength on Keira's part but because of her complete lack of hygiene, but that was Keira. If she had cared to, she could have gained great wealth and prestige as a court wizard; and advisor to kings, a merchant prince or even guild head. Not because mages of all sorts are rare today; you can't swing a cat, dead or otherwise, without hitting a spellcaster, but because she's *that good*. That and the fact that if she cared about her personal presence at all, she'd have her pick of suitors. But that wasn't Keira; like many of the book mages who actually could cast more than just rituals, Keira had issues. Not the least of which was not understanding why she should wash occasionally just because everyone else did.

"Sasha! How are you? Where's Miri? I know you're still with her because I can tell you two had sex last night," she said in a voice a drill sergeant would have been proud of.

I suddenly felt every eye turn towards me with far more interest than was proper. "She's outside with a new friend," I said in a quiet voice. As I did so I gestured to her to lower her volume.

Keira saw the gesture and her cheeks turned red in embarrassment. She then said in a much quieter voice "Sorry I'm just so excited to *see* you. Roland has a new contract and we've formed a new company to meet it. We're near full but I'm sure he'd never miss an opportunity to have two survivors of the Siliean plains join."

As she finished the young book mage's eyes finally registered Riley's presence on my shoulder. "Hello Riley I hope you're well," she said at a near whisper her eyes downcast. It was like she became a different person but being afraid of birds was just another Keiraisum.

"I am well; thank you Keira," said Riley with as much formality as I've ever heard from the bird.

I doubt the book mage actually heard him; having turned her full attention back to me. She asked her voice rising in volume once again. "Where are you staying?"

"We've a room in The Taleless Rat," I said.

"Roland and I know the place. We're having a dinner with the officers and senior specialists tonight. I'll have a carriage come at evening bell to pick you up. It will be so

41

nice to have some friendly faces at the table," she said, the speed of her talk increased as the idea formed in her head.

"Keira, you do remember that Miri and Roland didn't part on the best of terms don't you," I said cautiously.

"Oh, I'm sure that won't be a problem," replied the book mage with a degree of conviction I completely lacked.

Chapter Three

Once outside I noticed a small crowd had formed around Miri and Sariel. My love looked as if she was about to bolt in terror, but the Fey was drinking in the attention as if it were fine Elven Brandy.

But the Fey had kept enough of her wits to spot me exiting the blockhouse. "Well good people it appears that our leader has returned. I shall take all of your kind proposals to her and we shall get back to you as to our decision," she said to the surrounding group as she expertly flowed through their circle and moved towards me.

Miri started behind her but she moved so fast that she arrived first, two steps ahead of Sariel.

The Fey didn't seem to be phased by Miri's behaviour at all. "Four are ready to sign us up right now, and two others want proof of competency before we go further: and those are just the ones that are offering a hundred gold or more as a signing bonus," she excitedly said to me as she handed me several handbills.

Before I could take them, Miri grabbed both of us by the arm and started to quick march us back towards The Rat.

"They just surrounded her like wolves do a deer. As soon as she confirmed she was Fey they started making offers. Most were for dinner, until they realized that she was looking for mercenary work then all Nine Hells broke lose," reported Miri. "It's a good thing I fed last night, I wouldn't have been able to withstand the level of strong emotions that she generated otherwise."

"Miri, I do believe that you're exaggerating; granted I was trying to be gracious but everyone was civil," chided Sariel.

"If that was you just being 'gracious' I'd hate to see what would happen if you really turned it on. Sasha, I swear if I hadn't been their someone would have shanghaied her, and she be a 'cabin boy' on some galleon before you would have made it out of the Guildhall," said Miri as she 'escorted' us.

"But I'm not a boy..." started Sariel before she realized what Miri was talking about "Oh? Oh, that would be bad."

"Yeah *think*!" snorted Miri. Then taking a deep breath Miri turned back to me and said. "I hope you had some luck, because I'd not trust any of those offers until I check them out with a someone else.

"As luck would have it, I ran into Keira. She's still with Roland, and he's forming a new company and is looking for people," I said as I put the handbills into my great coat's pocket: always best to keep your options open. "We're invited to dinner tonight; a carriage is going to pick us up at evening bell," I said quickly, hoping that the matter of fact way I'd delivered the news would make Miri just accept the fact that we were going.

Unfortunately, I was wrong.

"And you agreed to all this without even asking me?" she said tartly.

Who are Keira and Roland?" asked Sariel curious.

"Roland was the commander of the mercenary company in which Miri and I met," I answered trying to put as positive a spin on the answer as possible.

"He was also the commander who got all but nine of his people killed in a war that could have been won," said Miri with a tone that clearly felt like an old scar opening.

"That wasn't his fault Miri, and you know it. The Prince who was paying us wouldn't listen and by the time we realized just how dangerous the situation was, it was too late," I replied, then added. "And he's also directly responsible for you being one of those nine."

"Which is why I'm not refusing outright," she said through gritted teeth. I could tell that Miri was having real problems with this. On the one hand, she had real difficulties with Roland for an issue that we had since learned through our own experience was a hard one for *any* sellsword to handle. With the other being the problem similar to that of your first love: you never forget it.

"You didn't agree to anything but dinner, right?" she asked finally.

"Only dinner, a free dinner I might add," I said reassuringly.

"A free dinner which will most likely have a shocking lack of eyeballs," complained Riley.

Chapter Four

Taking the fact that we were being picked up by carriage as a sign of the dinner being reasonably formal Miri and I decided to take the opportunity to 'dress' for the event.

The ritual preservation spells I had placed upon the one dress each one of us owned, had kept them both clean and reasonably unwrinkled in the bottom of our saddle bags was still intact. However, but both needed to aired out to get rid of the wet leather smell (ritual magic isn't one of my strengths).

The plan started to slip off the Old Empire Road, when Sariel became involved.

"You have dresses but what about everything else?" she asked.

"What everything else?" I asked with a level of innocence that had to be heard to be believe.

"Makeup, hairstyle, jewelry, shoes... You two don't have a clue as to what I'm talking about do you?" the Fey asked.

"We have a clue," replied Miri "Its just we've never really had an opportunity to exploit them."

"Until now that is! I've been sitting on my hands regarding your potential, but no more! Now it's time for a MAKEOVER," Sariel said excitedly.

Maybe it was the effects of the feeding or that Miri was, in part, Elven but she was swept up by Sariel's sudden mood change and readily agreed. I was, on the other hand, apprehensive. While I deal with the ebbs and flows of magic and combat easily, in personal affairs I tend to be more conservative. In part that's because being a wild mage already instills enough chaos in my life. The other part comes from being raised by a group of Dwarves who instilled a heavy dose of Dwarven morality and traditional values. But I could also tell that this was something that Miri really wanted to do and it is not often that my lover

46

really got excited about anything, so I agreed.

I started to regret that decision when Sariel used the magic locked into her left arm's tattoo and gemstones to open that magical portal of hers and she pulled out another sack. Inside this sack were two square boxes a foot aside. In one was a collection of paints, powders and brushes that even I knew were makeup. The other box contained half a dozen different hair brushes along with a whole bunch of things I didn't recognize.

Sariel started the ordeal by insisting that we rewashed our hair (we'd only washed it the night before why it needed to be washed again was beyond me) the Fey then set about, with far too much pleasure if you ask me, brushing braiding and in my case curling our hair.

"What about your hair?" I asked Sariel when she tied yet another lock of my hair up with a strip of cloth which she claimed would 'make my hair naturally curly for days'.

"Oh, that's easy," she replied and then with a single command word and a flick of her head her dull blonde hair became a cascade of golden tresses that reached down to her hips; and if that wasn't enough makeup suddenly appeared on her face making her eyelashes double in size, her lips become red highlighted to pink, and her cheeks a lovely rouge.

Riley squawked in surprise and Miri and I were so stunned that neither of us had time to feel at all jealous.

"If you can do that, why do you have all that," stuttered Miri pointing at the two cases.

"I'm going to want to change things at *some* point," Sariel answered as she approached Miri with a torture device disguised and as a hair brush.

Okay I might be exaggerating a bit about the brush but you have to keep in mind Miri and I grew up during the madness. While I was more fortunate than Miri being raised by Dwarves in Berg Provinz; neither of us had much time or instructors on what Riley often referred to as the 'feminine arts'. Oh, we both went through our 'independent' phase which is why both of us had a fair bit of body art, and the less said about 'mixed drinks' the better, but Sariel's makeover was a new experience for both of us.

But I couldn't argue with the results of the first phase. When Sariel was finished she produced a silvered mirror and I got my first look at her work. The volume of my hair had more than doubled; with the normal straight strands having been replaced with a cascade of silvery grey locks that reached down to between my shoulder blades. My grey eyes that always seemed to disappear into the general form of my face, were now surrounded by supporting lines of eye makeup, making them stand out.

When Miri saw the results; her eyes nearly popped out her head. Her reaction gave me the first sense of well 'girlish pleasure' that I've had in a long time. This pleasure was only magnified when I got a good look at what the Fey had done to her. Due to a constant need for a helmet to keep her alive in combat; Miri's hair had developed permanent 'helmet head' that she had long since tired of trying to fix. Sariel had taken this as a challenge, and had spent the sixty minutes it had taken to curl my hair; brushing out Miri's. Then deciding that 'keeping it simple' was best: Sariel had worked the Daywalker's hair into a single braid strategically place over her right shoulder. To this Sariel had changed the colour of a single lock of her hair from blood red to jet black. The Fey had then woven that lock through the braid as if it had been a black ribbon on the red background. Sariel had continued the black against red theme to Miri's makeup creating the Bard's stereotypical version the vampire vixen that my lover had almost constantly tried to live down, but today seemed willing to 'embrace'.

As both Miri and I expressed our almost embarrassed pleasure at Sariel's work; Riley expressed his opinion with a long wolf whistle.

"Riley!" I tried to be cross with him but mostly I was annoyed that I couldn't figure out how my Raven familiar could whistle without lips (yes, I know 'magic', but come on, sometimes you want a more detailed explanation than that.)

"As the only male in the room, I feel it necessary to express my gender's opinion on your appearances and Sariel's skill and hard work," he said loftily. "Especially given what she had to work with."

It says something about Miri's skill with throwing weapons that she was able to beam the Raven with a hair brush before he could move out of the way. With a squawk, the familiar quickly flapped behind a pillar and gave Miri an amazing lipless raspberry.

While it appeared that our hair and makeup were a success, and that Sariel was pleased with the results. The same couldn't be said when she took a good look at our dresses.

"You're serious? You both packed one dress each and these are what you chose?" she asked incredulous. "I mean I understand you're both sellswords and you're often away from the cities but still. Don't you have *any* fashion wizards in the Mid Reich?"

"Do you mean someone who designs and creates dresses or someone who actually uses magic to create the dresses?" I asked. One of the things that amaze me about the new world the Red Death had created was that despite people generally hanging onto life with their fingertips, and some new disaster arising every year ready to knock lose our hold; mortals still care about fashion. Not just care, but follow it with a zeal that you have to see to believe. As you can tell from my question, I lacked that zeal.

Sariel pinched the bridge of her nose in the mortal wide sign of a headache coming on. "Right: were meeting with someone who has enough power, money and influence to marshal together a second mercenary company after his first was destroyed. This is someone we want to put your best foot forward for, not to mention showing a bit of growth on your part to get a better deal. Let alone the potential of one or both of you becoming his mistress," she said taking charge.

"Actually," started Riley.

"Quiet bird brain: fairy godmother stuff happening right now," Sariel interrupted. "Well fairy godsister, but you get the idea."

Surprisingly my familiar did stop talking; and instead he just flew up to the rafters and relaxed waiting for the show.

"Right, now you're going to see some real magic," said Sariel as she went to her other box and pulled out a large piece of chock and two bolts of material. Turning back to the both of us, Sariel decided to go with Miri first, largely I imagine because of the dirty look I was still giving her after that 'real magic' remark.

"Miri, take off your clothing and any loose jewelry that you're wearing. Keep your body piercings though they might prove integral to the design I come up with," the Fey instructed as she created a chock circle upon the only open piece of wooden floor that remained in the room.

"*Design* the dress? Sariel I know I'm not an expert at all this but doesn't that take days to do?" I asked confused.

"So, you don't have fashion wizards in the Mid Reich then. Very well Sasha you're about to see some of the very best in ritual magic the Fey Reich has to offer," Sariel said with a dramatic flair.

Okay now this was starting to make sense. In all three realms, there are fundamentally two types of magic: spell magic and ritual magic. Spell magic is the quick channeling of magic energies, transforming them into physical matter and energy. It results could be mundane as creating a small candle flame, or mending a piece of cloth to as spectacular

50

as a fireball or ripping the earth itself open to swallow an enemy. This kind of magic can only be practiced by those who through accident, circumstance, or luck of birth can channel the magic through themselves.

Ritual magic on the other hand requires the use of magical trappings, such as circles, runes, and crystals: chants, songs and sometimes dance are also required. All of which takes time to prepare and preform; at least minutes, often hours and sometimes days in length. The main advantage of ritual magic however is anyone who has the time and patience can learn to cast them successfully. The ritual itself does all the work channeling the magic into a predictable result. What that result is can be as mundane or spectacular as spell magic.

Because of this power, prior to the Red Death, the instruction needed to cast ritual magic was limited to only the Wizard's Guild; the only organization that rivaled the churches in the Imperium and beyond.

Being a Wild Mage, thank you lightning storm, I came into my magic by accident. So I lack much of the formal training in the basics of magic that is considered a requirement of ritual casting. I can still cast them, with a little help from Riley, but they tend not to last as long or be as powerful as the rituals cast by someone from the Wizard's Guild.

Glancing down at Sariel's ritual though I could see that it was even sloppier than what mine usually were: but the power that it channeled. What it lacked in elegance it more than made up for in the amount of magic it could bring into focus. It was clear that Fairy magic theory was going in directions that Mid Reich practitioners hadn't even considered possible.

Just before she finished the circle Sariel got up and took a critical look at Miri's now bare physique. Even by human standards, Miri would have been considered muscular, with well-defined shoulders, arms and legs. But by Elven standards she was really brawny; to the point where many of her kindred thought that she had to be half-human. Her lean frame has also meant that some of her womanly features such as breasts are much smaller than even on a 'normal' Elf female. I thought she was perfect: but my opinion is biased. Over the layers of muscle Miri had covered herself with over a dozen tattoos of various sizes. Mostly on her arms and thighs but she did have one that covered most of the right side of her rib cage and another on the left collar bone.

As I have said before, tattooing, and other types of body art is common feature among younger sellswords, and like many of female adventurers, Miri has adopted the practice of tattooing the locations where a wound had been severe enough to leave a scar that our current healing could not remove. Apparently while 'chicks' may like scars; guys don't.

In my case, my scars were my tattoos: sort of. When the lightning bolt that made me a wild mage had struck, my body had been covered by a series of burn scars that looked like lightning bolt traveling down my torso and limbs. From what I've been told, from other survivors of a lightning strike (though no magical powers were gained in their cases) such scars were not uncommon but they usually faded in a week or two. Mine had been with me for four years and I suspect that I'll always have them.

"Your assets are amazing Miri," said Sariel snapping me back to the here and now. "Not what would normally be consider standard for an Elven woman. However, we're talking about sellswords so standard may not work in this case anyways," said Sariel who then snapped her fingers and said "Ah I know what will work."

With that Sariel handed Miri a cotton coloured smock and said, "Here put this on and step into the circle."

Miri might have been caught up by the Sariel's enthusiasm but paranoia is pretty standard for anyone hoping to get into their thirties. Before she followed Sariel's instructions she glanced over to me to see if I had any concerns.

"It's pretty standard for ritual work. It makes sense that you'd have to be inside the circle first. Otherwise you break the link between the ritual and the magic," I explained trying to relieve her fears. While I didn't lie to Miri, truth be told; I wanted to see how this ritual worked. So, I was as interested as Sariel was to get Miri in that circle.

Taking me at my word, Miri stepped into the circle which Sariel closed behind her. Once the circle was completed a smell of burnt air rose and my skin tingled the same way as it did before a big lightning storm. That circle was channeling *a lot* of power; a lot more power than I'd seen in the rituals created by masters like Keira, let along anything I could do. Despite Miri appearing completely fine inside the circle, *my* paranoia was starting to kick in.

"Right, first off, the dress," said the Fey as she made a small jester with her hands. Inside the circle the smock that Miri wore transformed: gaining length and tightly fitting around the Daywalker. When the transformation was done, Miri was wearing an ankle length dress that tightly fitted around her hips and waist. From where I sat I could see that the dress was backless, being held together by a long lace of material that had been tide tightly in such a way that it caused the front of the dress to actually support Miri's cleavage and giving her the illusion of more than was actually there.

However, what was even more striking was the complete lack of sleeves. Along with most of Miri's back, her arms and shoulders were completely bare showing off not only the defined muscle but her tattoo work as well.

"So, calf, mid-thigh, or hip?" Sariel asked me with a bored affect that completely contradicted what she had just done. Inside the ritual circle she had just created a dress, granted it was more of a transformation but still it wasn't an illusion but honest transformation; from a ritual, and as far as she told us; a completely untrained practitioner. I doubt Keira herself could have equaled that feat.

"Sasha: calf, mid-thigh or hip?" Sariel said again when I didn't reply the first time.

Crashing back to reality I said "Sorry Sariel; calf, mid-thigh, or hip what?"

"How high should the slit be in the dress?" the Fey asked as if the question was the most obvious thing in the world. "Never mind, we'll try hip first."

With that a long tear appeared on the right side of Miri's dress that exposed her entire right leg up to the hip. It was then that I noticed that Miri now wore a pair of ankle high boots with a five centimetre heel, down turned collar and curled toes. Actually I noticed a lot more, because more than just Miri's leg and foot were exposed when she moved more than a bit.

"Nice to see what is considered decent hasn't changed much since I was last in the Fey Reich," commented Riley.

"Too much?" asked Sariel with complete innocence.

"Yes!" Miri and I said in unison.

"Well, let's try mid-thigh then," the Fey said nonplussed. Then as if the tear had never existed Miri's dressed mended itself down to the middle of Miri's thigh.

"This works for me. I can move well and I'm not showing off things that people shouldn't be seeing on a regular basis," Miri said.

I had to agree. Overall the dress was a bit risqué, but I'd seen Elven women wear less, and compared to some of the cultists I'd seen Miri's dress was downright conservative.

Excellent now that we have the dress's shape we only need to decide on the colour," said Sariel as her right hand started to twirl in a circle. The dress turned the exact same blood red as Miri's hair.

"Okay no," Sariel said as soon as the colour registered.

Then the dress turned a bright snow white, which caused both Riley and I to comment, "Virgin white? Miri!"

"Point," Sariel conceded; and then the colour changes really began. With increasing speed, the dress changed into every colour I'd thought possible and quite a few that I never would have believed existed. There were bright blues, glowing yellows, and deep sea greens. Sariel's hand spun so quickly that I thought she would break her wrist. Finally, the colour changes stopped and the dress was back to the cotton colour it had started with.

With a large sigh, Sariel said as much to herself as anyone else, "this is what I get with starting with the makeup first," then to Miri she said, "I'm sorry Miri but there's only really one colour that going to work given the time we have left."

With that the dress and shoes turned a deep light stealing black that was so natural given Miri's hair colouring and makeup that I was surprised it hadn't been Sariel's first choice.

As if reading my mind, the Fey said, "Black works with so much that I always like to check everything else first even when it's obvious."

Holding up the mirror so that Miri could get some idea of what she was now wearing Sariel asked, "How do you like it?"

"I'm not sure, this is really the first time in years I've really played make-believe," my lover replied. She looked over to me desperate for an opinion that she could trust.

"I think you look gorgeous. It really plays on the sexy vampire trope a bit too much for a regular look; but tonight, I think it's safe for you to stand out," I said honestly.

"Oh, don't worry compared with what you're going to be wearing Miri, isn't going to stand out at all," said Sariel as she approached me with the second smock.

Chapter Five

Liza barged into the room to let us know that a carriage had arrived. "Miri, Sasha there's a covered carriage…" her voice trailed off as the spectacle of the three of us hit her.

"Oh wow!" followed by a squee of delight were the only sounds that came from Liza for a good thirty seconds.

"You two look fantastic. I hope you're going to a really posh party," she said finally speaking coherently.

"Dinner actually, but a reasonably formal one," I replied as I got used to walking in the skirt I now wore.

"We're about ready. Could you let the carriage know that we'll be there within ten minutes," said Miri as she gathered our great coats together.

The serving girl gave a very proper curtsy to Miri and then left the room.

"Here give me those," said Sariel as she took the two great coats and put them into a sack which then disappeared along with all the makeup back into the pocket dimension. "You're not going to need them until after the dinner anyways."

Sariel was back into her mercenary black and blues that she wore earlier today. Though now she was armed with a narrow-bladed dress sword, stiletto and two throwing spikes in the top of her calf high leather boots. She was to act as our 'escort' for the evening. Even though she dressed down, her hair and makeup would still cause heads to turn.

Around five minutes later, we left our room to quietly get to the entranceway and our awaiting carriage. As Sariel closed and locked the door, I heard Liza call for quiet from the top of the stairway. Apparently, Liza felt that since we looked like 'true ladies' we needed a herald. Standing at the top of the stairway she announced, "Gentlefolk and free peoples, may I present the ladies Sasha, and Miri on their first outing of the winter season."

Okay I've been the centre of attention before. I fling lightning bolts around like insults; such things tend to get noticed. Though to be fair the words 'kill the spellcaster' usually follow soon after acquiring all that attention. So when I turned the corner to descend the staircase into the main hall; and I felt every eye in the place on me the first thought that went through my head was: 'please oh please someone shout 'kill the spellcaster''.

Instead I was met with a stunned silence that lasted a full 10 seconds. Then every male in the place stood up (or was pulled to a standing position by their friends).

I had to remember to breathe. "Keep moving. Don't stop until were in the dining room," whispered Miri over her shoulder. Like she had to tell me; while her black dress enhanced her figure in all the right ways, at least it was completely opaque. For my dress Sariel had said that she was going for something truly Fae.

Inspired by the lightning scars, and my silver hair, the Fey had created what she called 'a walking art dress'. Styling my already curly hair into a fairly good approximation of a cloud she then added several silver hairclips that when they caught the light they really did look like a lightning flashing. My dress, while not as form fitting as Miri's, still attracted attention. Sariel had transformed it into something called gossamer. Depending upon how the light caught it, my dress was a light sky blue, light grey or transparent. The overall effect was that as I walked and people watched my movement it appeared that several bolts of lightning were coming from the clouds and down through a mostly clear day. For shoes, I wore a pair similar in design to Miri: only mine were a light grey in colour with silver lightning accessories and flat toes. Sariel assured me that only my arms and legs would show and not my more 'private' areas.

Even if I did flash too much skin, I wouldn't have really cared at this point. Miri, and I were the centre of attention in a positive way, i.e. no one was trying to kill us. Like many things in life it was scary at first, but by the time I was halfway through the room, I was rather enjoying the feeling, and as we were about to leave the common area, I had to suppress a giggle.

"I owe that Fey a big vote of thanks," whispered Riley in my ear as he landed on my shoulder.

"Oh?"

"Yes, it the first time in months that I've seen you genuinely happy," he said.

The feelings of happiness continued when we actually saw the carriage that Roland had sent to pick us up.

"Oh wow, Roland really did pull out all the stops with this one, didn't he," I said to my companions.

Painted white with gold inlay the carriage was pre-plague in origin, and showed all the majesty that forgotten era possessed. But what showed that Roland was trying to impress were the four matching white horses and the fact that the two footmen, and two drivers were not only dressed identically (in white and gold livery I might add) but they were all clean as well.

"Fraulein Storm Crow?" asked one of the footmen as we approached. His demeanor while polite was also confused.

"Yes, I'm her," I replied.

"My apologies Fraulein, we were told to expect three sellswords not two ladies and their escort," he said as he offered his hand to help us into the carriage.

I was glad for the help; moving with any degree of dignity in skirts takes some practice. The footman even helped Sariel up though she did have to put her hand out for him to get the hint.

"Well this is acceptable I guess," said Sariel as the carriage took off with a jolt.

I decided that I was enjoying being a princess too much, and didn't rise to the bait so I just let the Fey's comment lay. Though I had to admit, riding in the back of a carriage wasn't that much more comfortable than being in the back of a wagon. But it was only a twenty-minute ride and we all managed to survive with no bruises.

Chapter Six

Turned out, dinner was going to be served in a manner house which had been recently reclaimed from the ghosts of the noble family that had died there during the madness. This also explained where Roland had gotten his hands on such a fancy carriage: it had come with the house. As was common for recently reclaimed buildings it was covered in magical lights that prevented any shadows from being formed. The theory ran that without any shadows no energy from the Shadow Reich could build up: no shadow energy no ghosts. Along with the light spells every surface had either been scrubbed down to the raw stone or covered with several coats of fresh paint. All of these things were designed to show that new owners were in the house and that the ghosts were no longer welcome. Personally, I thought that was all a crock of shit but then I was a wild mage not a book mage; so, what did I know.

On the other hand, all the new surfaces and light really help to show off my dress and I glowed as I made my way to the buildings.

The front doors were open and only a liveried servant barred our entrance. That the servant was a battle-scarred dwarf with arms as thick as my waist meant the entrance was better guarded now than if the doors had been closed locked and barred.

"Fraulein Storm Crow?" he asked politely but with a firmness that indicated that there was only one answer that would gain us entry.

"Yes, and this is Miri and Sariel," I replied.

"Dressed for airs are we? Not what I'd expect from someone raised in a Berg orphanage," he said in Low Dwarf; his disapproval obvious.

I sighed, I loved my adopted people but their obsession with what was proper drove me nuts sometimes, but I long ago learned how to get around the old curmudgeons.

"Only old grey beards can get away with plate and leather for every occasion, even a proper lady dresses in lace sometimes," I replied in Low Dwarf as well. I then gave the Dwarf a chase kiss on the cheek. "But thank you for your concern elder."

The Dwarf turned a bright shade of red and grumbled something about young people before saying in Reich, "Drinks being served in the foyer; dinner will be called soon."

"What was that all about?" asked Sariel as we moved through the cloakroom and into the foyer. Inside there were at least thirty dinner guests and half as many servants. Of the guests, maybe twenty were sellswords of both sexes, and several races. All were mingling and most had vessels for holding alcoholic drinks of some sort.

"Oh, just an old Dwarf expressing his disappointment in the improper actions of a young Dwarf," said Miri.

"But Sasha's a human," Sariel said in puzzlement, as she grabbed three glasses of white wine from a passing tray and handed one each to Miri and myself.

"During the Plague, many of the Dwarf holds faced the very real concern that their race might become extinct like the Orcs. At the same time, they were horrified by the number of children of all races that were trying to survive on their own. So, they setup orphanages to house and feed all these children. The children grew up in a safe and loving environment; and the Dwarves hoped that while their race may die off the traits of hard work, community spirit and proper values, what made Dwarves, Dwarves in other words, would live on in their adopted children," explained Riley as the three of us tried the wine.

"So, they wanted to create a bunch of humans who wouldn't know what to do with something fun if it came up and slapped them? That's horrible," said Sariel.

"It was far better than hiding behind locked gates, or what many Elves continue to do," said Miri with a bitter tone.

Sariel was about to reply, when a familiar squealing voice warned us that Keira was incoming.

As I was enfolded by a pair of spindly arms I was surprised to see that Miri and I were not the only ones who had cleaned up for tonight's meal. Keira was in a *clean* dress whose boxy Dwarven cut, in the same shade of green that she all of her clothes were; did little to show off her features.

"Sasha, I hardly recognized either of you," she said as she turned and gave Miri an equally furious hug, which my lover carefully returned for fear of crushing the book mage.

"Where did you get the dresses? I've never seen their like before. They appear to be normal fabric but their infused with a type of magic that I don't…"

Her voice trailed off as her eyes dilated as she opened her senses to see fully into the spectrum of magic.

"Sasha you're wearing gossamer: your entire dress is gossamer! How did you afford? I'm not sure the Empress. There hasn't been since the Fey closed the portals," Keira's talking deteriorated into meaningless mumbling as she processed what she saw.

Then her eyes snapped up and for the first time she turned and looked over towards Sariel her magical senses still open.

"Sasha catch her," warned Riley.

Without thinking I moved forward and steadied the book mage as she let out a little cry, and swayed on her feet. With horror, I looked over the Fey wondering what she had just done, but Sariel was equally horrified by what had happened.

"She saw Sariel through her arcane sight. Seeing a Fey like that can be overwhelming to someone for the first time: especially a book mage," explained Riley.

I encouraged Keira to take a large sip of my wine as I kept the young woman on her feet.

"Is she alright?" asked Sariel her voice full of concern.

"Oh! That tastes offal!" sputtered Keira as the taste of the wine hit her brain. I smiled in relief, while something of a beer snob Keira can't stand the taste of wine.

"She's fine," Miri and I said together as Keira regained her feet, her magical senses closed by her eyes still wide with wonder. Turning towards Sariel she did a very reasonable curtsy to Fey saying something in what I believed was Imperial Elfish.

The Fey cocked an eyebrow in surprise and answered in what I think was the same language. Switching to Reich the Fey said to Keira "Your diction is very good, but you roll the 'R' a bit too long."

"I'll keep that in mind for the future Altus," replied Keira; still excited her voice growing louder with each passing word.

"Oh, I'm no noble, mage, please just call me Sariel, and you are?" replied the Fey extending her hand in greeting.

"Keira, my name is Keira, personal aide and chief magical support to Captain Roland," she said as she shook the Fey's hand.

Looking around I was horrified to realize that yet again (you think that I'd be getting used to this) everyone in the room was looking our way. Fifty or so sets of eyes were now focused on us. Even the dozen or so servants in the room had stopped and were looking. Then I realized that they weren't annoyed with Keira's drill sergeant's voice carrying through the room, everyone was looking at me and my two companions. Miri and I because of our appearance and Sariel because she was the first Fey many had ever seen in their lives. For several seconds, no one moved: even Keira fell silent. Then everyone who was staring realized that I had caught them in the act and now no one knew what to actually do next. Finally, the moment passed as a young sellsword dressed in a clean though wrinkled tunic and hose came forward and introduced himself. "Good evening Fraulein, I'm Heinrich, I apologise for staring, it just that you stand out so much in that dress, I've never seen it's like. Is Fraulein Keira correct and your dress is made from gossamer?"

He was one of those men who knew he was handsome and was used to using it as an advantage in most social situations. He was also experienced enough to switch to a plan B when he didn't get the gushing reaction that he was expecting.

"I'm not sure: you'll have to ask Sariel: she's the one who made it," I replied in a neutral tone as I pointed towards the Fey.

Looking over towards my friend he said, "Ah so Keira was also correct in that as well: your companion is from the Fey Reich?"

That comment caught me a bit unawares and then I thought about it for a second. Sariel was the first Fey I'd met. Why had that never occurred to me before this moment? As I thought about it I couldn't remember any conversation between Miri, myself and Sariel about where she was from. For that matter, I don't think we'd ever had a talk as to how and why she'd ended up in the Mid Reich in the first place. All that we knew about her past was that she had ended up chained to the gallows because she rejected the advances of the head of a Demon Cult, and that was it. Strange, spend several days let alone over two weeks riding with someone you normally ended knowing their entire life story, and then some. It simply helped pass the time. Yet I couldn't recall a single conversation about Sariel's past. Oh, I could recall several long conversations where both, Miri and I talked about growing up, our adventures and the history and state of the Imperium. Hells even Riley had gotten into the story telling. Yet it had always been Sariel asking the questions. I guess she just didn't have that interesting of a life. Putting that thought out of my head, I returned my attention back to Heinrich.

I was about to say something when a major gong rang out and another uniformed servant cried out "Ladies and Gentleman dinner is served."

"Ah, a question for another time: Fraulein Storm Crow, may I escort you to your chair," said Heinrich extending out his arm.

Without really thinking about it, I took his arm and walked into the dining room.

Behind me I heard Sariel say her voice full of mirth "Fraulein Miri could I *escort* you to your chair."

"You'd better or I might not get to eat at all," said my lover in a rather neutral tone.

Chapter Seven

Given the size of the manor, the dining room was a little on the small side; but it was still large enough to comfortably seat the thirty or so officers and technical staff that made up Roland's command elements. Like the rest of the manor, the room had been freshly painted and redecorated to suit its new owner's tastes. This translated into a long central table lit by many tall spermaceti candles instead of a large central chandelier with enchanted crystals giving off light. Along the walls were a collection of mounted weapons and shields denoting Imperium's long military tradition.

Despite moving into the room as part of the crowd, Roland had no trouble spotting us.

"Sasha! Miri! I'm so glad to see you both again. And if it's not to bold; I do not believe I've ever seen you both look lovelier. But who is the young lady with you? I don't believe I've had the pleasure," said Roland as we moved into the room, looking for our seats. As usual his voice was as flat as one that came from a magic mouth spell; and of course, his features didn't change as he spoke. From past experience, I'd learned that Roland was a very honest person and that it was best to take his words at face value.

What was really surprising was that for the first time that I'd known her Sariel: found something within the Mid Reich that actually impressed her.

I guess a bit of context is needed here. In the first year of the plague, it had become clear that any mortal creature (including the most ancient Dragons) could not only contract the Red Death but die from it as well. However, the real kicker was that the divine intervention that for centuries had shielded people from disease, starvation and so many other evils failed when mortals needed the help the most. The plague couldn't be cured and those that died from sickness couldn't be raised. While the God's duplicity in the plague's tragedy directly led to The Great Betrayal during the years of madness it also had the side effect of forcing a lot of book mages to look for alternatives.

One of the most radical of these alternatives was created by Gregory of Strasburg. One of the most powerful wizards in the Central Provinces, Gregory was a master at the creation and control of golems. Seeing the potential end of the world, he hit upon the idea of creating a special golem that could house a mortal soul. After months of failures, the wizard finally succeeded in transferring a soul of a gifted military officer, who was in the early stages of the disease, into his first prototype golem body. Then in a twist of fate that only a Bard could think of, Gregory died of plague himself. None of the local book mages could understand the rituals let alone duplicate the result. Only Gregory's young apprentice understood enough of the basics to even do maintenance on the golem to keep its magically complex systems operational.

After the human/golem hybrid got his mind wrapped around what he was, he decided that the world was going to be in need of every good military officer that they could lay their hands on. So, taking the apprentice, a young girl barely past her tenth year named Keira, under his wing he started to hire himself out as a mercenary captain.

To sum up: the Roland that Sariel met wasn't a Human, Elf, Dwarf or even a Hobgoblin but a six foot six self-aware golem made of steel, leather and whalebone. Normally he wore a specially constructed suit of plate armour, but it appeared that Miri and I weren't the only ones who decided to have a change of pace; as Roland wore what appeared to be a noble's tunic and hose over his mechanical frame.

"Roland may I present Sariel of the Fey Reich, we met only a couple of weeks ago; yet we've all become friends since then.

"Milady," said Roland has he knocked his heels together and gave the Fey a formal bow from the waist. "I

67

take it you are responsible for our two ducklings transformation into swans?" he asked in perfect Court Elven.

"They were always swans my lord they've just decided to reveal it tonight," replied the Fey without missing a beat.

Glancing over Sariel's shoulder to the large crowd behind us, Roland said, "Whatever the case, I believe on behalf of every male in the room I owe you a vote of thanks."

"Already have that one covered Roland," said Riley with a wink.

Roland barked out a laugh and then turned and addressed the room: "Please everyone have a seat this is not only a supper but a chance for everyone to get to know each other in a more relaxed setting."

As we moved to the table Roland gallantly held out the seat for both Sariel and Miri. Heinrich pulled back a seat for me, but his seat was between Miri and me. I gave him a disproving look, "Sorry Heinrich I'm taken," I said as I pulled out what was to be his seat and sat down next Miri. Heinrich took the slight in a good light and gave a slight victory nod to Miri and sat down in the chair he'd pulled out for me.

Once we were all seated, and the first course of our meal was brought out, vegetable soup with a dark rye bread and bottles of the local white wine (and a small stein of beer for Keira). Roland; who couldn't eat, took advantage of everyone else stuffing their faces to start explaining the contract.

"We've been hired by the Prince of Ulm for a six-month contract to reinforce his personal forces against what he expects to be several incursions from the Titan Spawn within the mountains west of his lands. It's been a cool summer in the region and while his land's crops were sufficient for his own needs past experience indicates to the prince that the Spawn in the mountains are going to be hungry and resorting to raiding to feed themselves," said Roland.

"Is the expectation that our role is purely defensive or are we going to be able to take the initiative this time?" asked Miri. While her tone was neutral, my lover's question still had plenty of barbs. When we'd last fought with Roland, we'd been restricted to a purely defensive operation. So despite seeing signs of the Phoenix Republic preparing for a major attack we'd done nothing about it. Something that Miri believed lead to the defeat and our near death.

"This time Miri I've made sure that we have a free hand to take the initiative. We can take offensive action if and when it benefits our main mission," replied Roland; who then continued answering questions from his other officers. As the main course of seasoned cod over rice was served I realized that I was pretty impressed by both the questions that were being asked to Roland and the answers he was giving. They were specific and mostly logistics based. Like Miri I'd learned a lot about working as a sellsword and that it was as important to know what kind of questions to ask about a contract as much as the sort of answers you wanted to here. Both were happening right now which gave me confidence that we weren't signing onto another disaster.

But it wasn't just conversation that impressed, the food was excellent and the wine flowed freely, and while it wasn't the tradition of the Imperium Provinces along the Great Green to make sure your guests were drunk by the end of the night; everyone at the table were well into their cups. Roland's review of the contract and the following question and answer period had ended: it was time for more mingling. Every gentleman at the table (and several of the women as well) had come up with an excuse to talk to Miri, Sariel or myself; and more than a few had managed to come up with a reason to talk to all three of us sometime during the night. I had received invitations to coffee, drinks, dinner, and one serious question as to how 'open' my relationship with Miri was. I was able to maneuver my way through them all without actually saying yes to anything but without bruising any fragile male egos. Through it all Sariel kept up with the self-proclaimed role as our social protector. Her abilities to change social roles fascinated me. At the blockhouse, this morning she had come off as the consummate flirt gaining many promises but giving none in return. Now the Fey was the skilled diplomat; she listened to the many conversations directed to all three of us, and defected or redirected the inappropriate questions away or towards herself. Once she heard that I could handle myself in this social situation, she concentrated on running interference for Miri whose social skills were not suited for polite defence. It wasn't that she lacked social skills, but they were geared far more to 'social offence' for lack of a better term. She was a Daywalker, and her social skills were far more suited to seducing a suitable meal to a secluded corner and feeding, than politely turning down invitations. Sariel's running interference kept everyone in a positive frame of mind and unbitten.

Of course, it was when all the dinner guests were focused on other pursuits that the Demon Cultists attacked.

Chapter 8

Demons have a reputation of being chaos incarnate; there actions being so unpredictable that mere mortals could never anticipate when or where the attacks would come. Their believers have traded upon this reputation to the point that the mere mention of a Demon Cult being in the area can spread panic and terror among a mortal community.

The truth is a *little* different. Oh, Demons are scary and tough to kill. However, their preferred method of attack had changed little since the cults rise during The Madness, and there *always* was a component to any of their actions which corrupted the local flow of magic.

Now Book Mages, like Keira, might have a better understanding of the flows of magic around them and in theory get more information from their examination: but they have to open themselves to the magical currents. They have to be looking for trouble in other words to see it.

Wild Mages, like yours truly, interact with the magical energy of the world on a much more intuitive level. We passively interact with it constantly. We *feel* the magic flow around us. So, when their attack began I felt the magic being corrupted precious seconds before they could take physical action.

The attack was a combination of demonic possession and transformation. In a magical ritual a piece of a Demon is implanted into a willing volunteer. Then several hours later, or at the pronouncement of a command word, the Demon transforms (emerges from?) their mortal host into a rage filled killing machine.

I was hit by the magical disruption of three of these rituals simultaneously; causing me to gag in response.

"Demons!" I managed to cry out as I rose unsteadily from my seat. Before the Red Death, most mortals reacted to the bladder emptying terror of a Demon by either fleeing in blind panic or freezing in place unable to move; and

71

truth be told since the Red Death many mortals still react in those two ways. However, post plague; many of us have personal Demons that are far scarier than any physical Demon we may encounter. When faced with such physical Demons our instinctual response is to attack. All I needed now was to locate the targets.

Looking around I saw one server, a girl who was in her teens, in the processing of vomiting a Demon into existence. Her jaw had dislocated and much of her head's soft tissue was already torn apart as a lizard headed Demon with three fingered claws pushed itself from its former host.

A part of me wretch at the site and for a moment I regretted the third glass of wine.

'Throw up later, right now kill that thing before its ready,' hissed the sellsword part of my mind. Then with a discipline born of constant hours of practise I opened myself to the magic and forced the raw energy into a bolt of electrical energy. I then flung the energy towards the two still combined bodies. Without Lightning my attack wasn't as accurate but at twenty feet I couldn't really miss.

The lightning caught the Demon dead centre, the creature screamed in pain and what remained of the serving girl convulsed as the lightning caused all of her muscles to contract. This had the unfortunate effect of ejecting the Demon from her body reducing her to an empty bag of skin.

Fortunately, I was too focused on killing what she had given birth to, to really notice. I followed up my first bolt of lightning with a second and third: striking the Demon while it tried to get to its feet. My attacks slowed the creature but I wasn't able to unleash my full power against it for fear of hurting the other mortals within the room. However, the attacks were powerful enough for me to start feeling the backlash. The fingers on my right hand were burned a bright red and the scars along the back of my hand and forearm looked fresh and in two areas had started to bleed. This was the other reason why I used Thunder and Lightning; they channelled the magic better and greatly reduced the effects of backlash I would normally take.

"Sasha right!" shouted Riley breaking me of my tunnel vision centred on the Lizard Demon.

Just in time I turned and saw the second Demon, a mind warping mixture of a bear and Ogre as it smashed its way through mortals and the table to get at me. It was a fast and powerful creature but when I take in the magic my own reflexes become 'lightning' quick as well.

Instead of striking the big demon with another bolt of lightning, I gathered up as much air around me as I could in the second I had before the Demon's bear like claws could rake me open. I then released the air in a thunderous blast that rammed into the creature's chest, matting its bear like fur against its body and stopping the Demon dead in its tracks.

The attack only bought me a couple of seconds as the large creature shook off the effects of the spell. Screaming its annoyance at me, the Demon raised its clawed arm to strike me down.

But those two seconds were all that Keira and Roland needed. Suddenly the bear/Ogre Demon was bound in what appeared to be a silver/blue coil of barbed wire. The wire cut deep through both bear fur and Ogre like skin and into Demon flesh releasing black blood. Unable to move, the creature bellowed as much in pain as surprise with its imprisonment.

This roar was matched by Roland's as loud, though much tinnier pitched, battle cry. The metal golem had jumped onto the table and in a running tackle slamming his weight into the larger monster knocking it onto the ground is a mess of chairs and serving dishes. Pulling his right arm back I noticed that our commander now sported a twelve-inch stiletto like blade from the back of his right fist.

'Keira must have been upgrading him again," the more

73

academic part of my mind commented, as Roland slammed the blade into the back of the Demon's head just above the neck's connection. Driving the steel deep into what passed for the Demon's brain. The other worldly creature convulsed once and lay still.

Turning back to finish dealing with lizard Demon I saw that Heinrich and Sariel had that one well in hand. The creature was on the ground pierced by half a dozen of the Fey's throwing spikes. Where Sariel had concealed them, I have no freaking idea. Heinrich was now over the creature bashing its head with a heavy candle stick while my fairy godsister, dress sword in hand, was stabbing it in every open space she could find.

Quickly looking around I realized someone was missing. "Riley! Where's Miri?" I shouted to my familiar. Were both short even compared to other women and right now the dining room was chaotic jumble of much larger bodies.

That she wasn't in my line of site during a fight sent a chill down my spine. Yes, Miri is more than capable of taking care of herself but we're better as a team.

"Other side of the table, she's keeping a third Demon busy letting others escape," came his reply from the rafters.

Hiking up my dresses' skirt, I started to run around the table: cursing the entire time as I tried to worm my way through the mass of people who were trying to *get out* of the room. I have several spells that can increase my speed and even allow me to fly. But they were useless inside an even large room like this one. As were most of my combat spells; yes, I can cut lose with small bolts of energy but my more powerful spells had too great a chance of hurting innocents.

Finally, I was able to catch site of my black and red lover. As Riley had said she was playing mongoose to a wolf headed snake Demon's well snake. She had managed to rip a six-foot battle sword from its wall mounting and

74

was more than holding her own against the Demon.

"Down lass!" boomed a distinctly Dwarven voice from the other side of the entrance way. Seeing that they now had a clear field of fire, half a dozen servants armed with muskets, and a book mage cut lose with shot and spell. A beam of cold struck the Demon slowing its movements which allowed four of the muskets to hit their mark. Seventy calibre balls tore into and out of the Demon upper torso causing what remained intact to collapsed into a bloody heap. The Dwarf doorman and several other house guards emerged from the dining room's entry way; tap loading their firearms and looking for any other threats.

"There were only three, and we got them all," I said to the Doorman.

"While I'm inclined to believe you lass, we'd ask that everyone move to the foyer while we sweep the house for more threats," he replied grimly.

I usually find it smart to comply with a polite request of musket armed servant but I was interrupted, by my feelings being overwhelmed once again by the rotting smell of demonic magic, but I'd felt this kind of magic before and suddenly I knew who we were dealing with.

"Everyone stop!" I shouted as the snake Demon started to clearly laugh despite most of its lungs not being there and more. It rose up like a puppet on a string, casting shadows far too large for the size of its body. Dead eyes staring right me.

"Hello Misery," I said knowing who I was speaking with.

"Ah so the Storm Crow recognizes me, does she? Good, good it is proper that the condemned should know who her executioner is," said Misery.

"So, this is the way it's going to be, is it?" I asked trying to keep my voice as flat as possible. I wasn't going let this Demon know just how scared I was right now.

"You two killed one of mine, and robbed me of a

sacrifice. Weregild must be paid for such an offence," said Demon.

"You and yours have no power to collect Demon. Let it go; or we'll destroy every follower you have within the Reich," I said. Miri didn't say a word but she rested her newly liberated battle sword causally across her shoulder and gave the Demon a toothy grin her fangs down to emphasise the point. We weren't scared by his treats.

Misery was about to say something but Keira decided end this conversation once and for all. There was a flash and suddenly smell of gun oil and steel filled my nostrils as the Book Mage's banishment spell took effect.

Not only did the Demon collapse back into a dead body, but all three of the creatures burst into flames burning themselves to nothingness while not damaging anything around them. It that was because of Keira than she'd increased in power since the last time we'd met as well.

No one moved until the last of flames died out.

"Well Sasha it appears that you three have been targeted by a Demon Cult," said Roland calmly as he looked at the carnage that had once been his dining room.

"It looks that way," I replied.

"Well it best course of action for you then would be join a large body of armed individuals who are heading out of town as quickly as possible," he said his voice as always unemotional.

"I agree. It's a good thing we were already doing that," I said back to our commander.

"Ah but there's the problem you three actually hadn't signed the formal contract. Now I'm more than willing to still have you sign on but given the risk we're going to running I'm afraid that compensation will not be as generous as it could have been before this *incident*," Roland replied.

I groaned Roland had us over a barrel, this attack just

blew our chances with any other mercenary company for the season, and we'd be lucky to get half what we were worth with Roland now. Damn Misery! Why couldn't he have waited to attack until after we'd signed the contract!

Pagan Winds

Chapter 1

Along with magic, or maybe because of it, our world is full of spirits. The book mages and other scholars have organized them into categories and gave them names: like Air, Earth, Bear, Fox and Raven (don't get Riley started on that last one). These categories work for smaller spirits however, the larger more powerful ones are the embodiment of chaos itself and defy such classifications. These more powerful spirits are either drawn to, or create, depending on which book mage you talk to, the natural phenomena of our world.

Ruling over this numberless collection of spirits are the Titans: also called the Primordials, the Old Ones or any number of puffed up ominous names. These immensely powerful spirits are thought to have created the world and everything that inhabited it. And like anyone who creates something the Titans think of the world as theirs, and that they're allowed to change it at their whim. It doesn't help that many of the Titans like 'playing' with mortals. History is full of stories, songs, and epic poems about how this Titan or that one destroyed a town in a flood or an earthquake because the mortals had 'offended' it; or how they transformed the entire male population of a town into pigs; just as a joke.

Then around a thousand years ago the Gods arose out of nowhere. Saying that they were on the side of mortals, they entered into an agreement with us known as the Covenant. Long story short the Heavens War resulted from the agreement, and though the war lasted less than a year the world was forever changed. It was split into the Three Reichs of Fey, Mid and Shadow; the Titans and those insane enough to follow them, were forced into the wild regions of all three Reichs, and the vast majority of Mortals and the Gods worked together to build a 'better' world.

And by and large they succeeded. Everyone I know who was alive before the Red Death said that the quality of life rose quickly. Manipulating magic and with the help of the Gods, mortals understood how the world worked more than ever before. I mean how would we have ever have discovered germs and their links to disease if it hadn't been for divination magic? Even given the rose-coloured glasses that many looked at that time with, it's clear that people had enough to eat, were reasonably clothed and sheltered and were generally happier then they ever before.

But then came the Red Death. This and the years of madness that followed showed us the folly in trusting the word of a God too far. They broke the Covenant and now without their aid, the Titans are on the rise again flexing their muscles and expecting mortals to knuckle under.

I say once burned, twice shy to that idea. Maybe it was my Dwarf up bringing but I'll never bend my knee to another being, mortal or otherwise 'just because'.

"So this is what being cold feels like? Can't say that I'm particularly fond of the feeling," complained Sariel as we scouted ahead of the main column.

Though sometimes; I think about reconsidering that position.

"But, all the different colours of the leaves and the crispness of the air almost make it worthwhile," she added; making me shift immediately back to my original position regarding worshiping other things.

"See, I told you that this would be worth getting up early for," I said cheerfully pulling my horse next to hers.

"Since Roland ordered us on this patrol, it wasn't like we had a choice," said Miri her mood surly. My Daywalker lover hadn't fed since Liza in the Taleless Rat three weeks ago and her mood was getting more depressed and negative with each passing day.

We had stopped on a small crest overlooking the Old Empire Road that would take our mercenary company to

80

our current employer. Beyond the road was a hardwood forest that was nearing the end of its fall colours; many of the leaves had already fallen but it was still brilliant enough to give our mercurial Fey some pleasure.

Despite my levity, I secretly didn't share my friend's joy at the site of the forest. This was the outer fringe of The Titan's Wald. Twenty years ago, this had been cultivated and prosperous farm land that along with feeding the Principality of Ulm had fed two free cities and an Wizard's Guild 'research centre'. But, that was again, before the Red Death. I feel like I am repeating myself, nevertheless when an event, directly or indirectly, lead to the death of two thirds of the mortals living in the three Reichs, it hard not to use it as a benchmark for well everything.

Anyways, the plague hit the region hard, and after it burned itself out, perhaps one in five of the original inhabitants remained on the land. A group of Titan worshipers, known within the Imperium as the Pagans, started to migrate into the area the next year: and that was when things got really bad. While the Imperium was deep in the grip of the Madness the Pagan's druids channelled the Titan's power (they know the beings as 'The Old Ones') to take control of the living earth to revert it back to the heavy thick forest that had covered it back in the days of the Old Empire. This in turned allowed the spread of the Titan's influence back into what used to be the heart of the Imperium.

Only the Old Empire Road, with its magical protection and preservation spells wrought in every pebble, resisted the Druid's magic and remained intact. It was this road that our company had to traverse to get to Ulm before the winter snows cut us off from the Southern Provizes.

On either side of the road, for about one hundred metres lay our destination; the village of Letzte Moglichkeit. The village, surrounded by a stout wood and gravel wall, had sprung up soon after The Titan's Wald. It served as the last piece of civilisation on the before plunging into the unnatural forest.

Roland had ordered Miri, Sariel, and I to make contact with the village leaders and let them know that a large mercenary company was soon going to pass through. If they had any provisions to sell we would be interested in purchasing them. Otherwise we'd just make camp outside the village walls and then start our way through the Titan Wald at dawn's light tomorrow.

Why us? You may ask. Well as Roland put it "hearing that you're being put upon by a bunch of mercenaries is easier to take coming from a trio of pretty young women than a two and half metre-tall mechanical man."

While he had a point, I just hope that we would be as well received as Roland. He might be intimidating, but at least people listened to him.

At least this time we wouldn't stand out very much from ordinary travellers. Before we had left Florenz, Sariel had made herself several sets of Imperium travel clothing. Well I had actually made the clothing, practicing with the dress making ritual she had used to make my and Miri's dresses. And while one of the pairs of pants had been a bit too long in the leg and another a little tight in the butt, and all the shirts were a size to small and showed off the Fey's cleavage just a bit too much to be proper; the Fey hadn't been unhappy with the results.

One thing I hadn't created for her was the outer wear. She had finally agreed to get a reinforced great coat similar to mine and Miri's and her own beaver felt tricorne hat. To top off her more Mid Reich look Sariel, had accessorized with a brace of flintlock horse pistols and a smoothbore flintlock carbine, keeping a dozen prepared paper cartridges in a rubberized box on her saddle as far from me as possible.

In a last note of defiance however she had magically coloured all of the clothing and the weapon's wood work flat black to stand out.

Miri and I were armed pretty much as we usually were me with my magical stilettos Thunder and Lightning hooked to either side of my great coat and Miri with her usual Old Empire short sword and dagger around her waist and her longsword on the right side of her horse. Given the more open terrain that we had been traveling through, Miri had pulled out her Hobgoblin composite bow and twenty-five broad head arrows for some extra range. Normally the bone, wood and horn bow would have fallen apart in the damp fall weather, but Miri had long ago had me put a water repulsing enchantment on the bow. Because it was a weather-based ritual I'd been able to cast it with enough power that it kept the bow whole and I'd not had to recast it in the two years she'd owned the weapon. Roland might not have meant us to greet the locals as heavily armed as we were, but in her short time on the Mid Reich even Sariel had learned the importance of a woman going around armed and appearing competent.

As we road openly down the Highway, I noticed a distinct absence of farmers in the fields. Oh, the fields looked well-tended; in fact, several looked as if they were in the middle of harvesting. However, the people who were supposed to be tending those fields were nowhere to be seen. Glancing up, I tried to spot Riley, my raven familiar. He had been flying above the village scouting; he might have an idea of what was going on. So, I was concerned when I saw his black form flapping hard towards me. At that speed he was going to have a hard time landing on my shoulder. So, I held out my arm and he quickly switched course and landed there: gripping the arm with his claws hard enough that I was thankful for my leather coat.

"We've got trouble!" he said once he had caught his breath.

"Define trouble?" I asked.

"Pagans: around thirty of them. They've gathered the

entire village in the central commons and it looks as if they're forcing them to cast lots. For what; I don't know.

I looked to Miri and Sariel. "What do we do?"

"I know of only one reason why Pagans have people draw lots," said Miri pulling her longsword loose in its sheath. A rising tone of anger and an anticipation of a fight made it clear what her opinion was.

"Sacrifice," I agreed.

"The Mid Reich's Titan followers practise mortal sacrifice?" asked Sariel.

"Yes, and almost any other vile mortal practise that you can imagine. The Titans blackmail them into doing whatever they find amusing. If they don't, the most merciful of them simply curse them with a flood, fire or earthquake: the others get creative," I said. Like Miri I have little time a Titan's followers.

"So, I take it we're going to try and stop them from taking the villagers for sacrifice?" she asked.

Miri and I just nodded in agreement.

"I can agree to that," Sariel said as she pulled out her carbine from its saddle sheath. Making sure the primer pan was full; she laid the smoothbore weapon across her lap and proceeded to start to move forward.

I gestured for Riley to hop onto my shoulder and then spurred my horse to catch up to Sariel. Miri maneuvered her mount between us. It was never a good idea for me to get too near gunpowder, especially when I was intentionally casting spells. Gunpowder and lightning do not react well when mixed.

As we rode onto the village commons I saw that Riley's description was pretty much right on target. It appeared that the entire village had been herded into the centre of the commons and surrounded by a group of fur covered Pagan woodsmen armed to the teeth. Most were armed with poorly forged iron weapons red with rust, but a had better-quality steel weapons that looked as if someone was at least pretending to look after them. Here and there an individual carried a flintlock musket or old-style arquebuses, their burning matches giving away their positions.

At the centre of the crowd was a slightly raised platform on which stood several better dressed Pagans, (meaning that the furs they wore were nowhere near as oily as those worn by their followers) what looked to be the village headman and around five women all of which were old enough to bear children. Surrounding the platform was another line of woodsmen. Like their companions on the outer circle, they were focused on the villagers. From the distance that I was observing them, all the villagers appeared to be tense and clearly close to violence. The villagers obviously didn't like what was happening, but they appeared helpless to stop it.

"Ah this isn't a call for sacrifice, it's a bride raid," said Miri sourly.

"A what raid?" asked Sariel.

"Bride raid, these Pagan cocksuckers obviously don't have enough of their own women to produce the children they need to keep their numbers up, so their steeling the village's women," I explained. My anger rising, I spurred my horse forward and maneuvered him so that I would be in direct line of sight with one of the Pagan leaders. If they wanted women: let's see how much they wanted three who could fight back.

It didn't take us long to find out. I'll give the speaker credit; many blowhards love the sound of their own voice so much that their entire world shrinks to just themselves. This one appeared to see us coming before any of his guards did and without missing a beat of his speech alerted them to our presence. Once alerted; six of his followers broke off from keeping the villagers in line and started to approach us.

Glancing over towards Miri I motioned my head ever

so slightly to the hitching posts in front of the village's blacksmith. Appearing to ignore the possible threat that the six woodsmen presented, we cantered our horses over to the posts. As we did so I whispered to Riley "Get back to Keira and tell her what's happening. We need all the dragoons and as many soldants still with the main body here as soon as possible."

"Sasha, I'm not comfortable…" he started to reply.

"Just do it, Riley. We'll be fine but we need the support," I said cutting him off.

"Keep your eyes," he said as he took off heading south with a speed that a hawk would have been impressed with.

Miri and I have unfortunately, have had to handled other groups that had seen women as only breeding stock. We've come up with what Roland would call a 'standard operating procedure'.

"Follow my lead," Miri said to Sariel as she dismounted and worked her way around her horse to that it was between her and the Followers. Sariel; for once, did as she was told and followed Miri, leaving me to face the six followers alone.

As usual I kept my bearing as neutral as possible, I acknowledged that the Pagans were coming towards us but I wasn't that worried about them. They stopped about ten feet away and just stood there for a good fifteen seconds waiting for a response. I let them wait.

Finally, their leader broke the silence "Good morning," he said in a deep rumbling voice that wasn't unpleasant to hear. In a flash of inspiration, I realized that he would have an excellent singing voice.

"Morning," I said acknowledging him for the first time. Standing at least two metres tall, he was the very definition of a bear of a man, and he made bears seem small by comparison. Despite the morning chill, I saw that while he wore rough linen pants and leather boots, his upper body was only covered by a bear fur vest. The vest did little to hide his own thick body hair or the blue/black tattoos that marked him clearly as a bearshirt. This meant that he was an extremely dangerous man, well that and the bearded war ax that looked like it weighted eight kilos that he hefted easily in his right hand.

"Are you nearly done?" I asked as I pointed back towards the Common.

"Pretty soon. Join us: there is lots of room for you and your friends," he said, an edge of steel entering his otherwise still outgoing voice.

"Yeah I don't think so. I'm not really interested in spitting out half a dozen kids; not to mention all that's implied in getting those six brats in the first place," I said my tone still light.

"I'm afraid that I wasn't asking. My group's leader is expecting you to join us," he said with what appeared to be genuine regret. But that didn't stop him from hefting up his ax or his followers from getting their weapons ready. I also felt a sudden wave within the magic energies around me, and I realized that he was literally breathing in the local magic. His features started to change, becoming hairier and his height and bulk growing.

"You're a bearshirt aren't you? Is it true that you can only be harmed by magic?" I asked though I already knew the truth.

"For the most part; I'm plenty hard to kill. I've taken the fire of an entire Imperium musket line before I tore them apart," replied with only a bit of boosting. His words were surprisingly clear given that his lower jaw had just sprouted two very bear like canines.

"Oh. Well this really isn't your day then," I said with all the sympathy I could muster. I grabbed Thunder's hilt pulled it from its sheath and, unleashed the spell I'd readied since I saw the Pagans walking towards us.

A whirling cyclone of air whipped down around the bearshirt striking his compatriots and throwing them back 5

87

metres. The ground was still in the shade of the forest and so still hard from the overnight freeze so Pagans landed on what felt like stone. One was armed with a matchlock which discharged harmlessly into the air: the sharp crack of the weapon lost to the howl of the winds my spell created around him.

It was one of my more powerful spells, and even with Thunder helping to channel the magic energies, I still felt a trickle of blood from my right eye as the backlash hit. The strain had been even more because I had gotten fancy and left the bearshirt standing in the eye of the mini tornado.

Once again I was the centre of attention as every eye in the village both friendly and hostile turned to see what had made that great and completely unexpected noise.

The bearshirt gave the pretty much standard reaction to being on the receiving end of one of my spells.

"Mage," he said with enough relish to make clear that he thought I was now worthily of his attention. He'd finished is transformation; adding twenty-five centimetres to his height and about ten kilos of fur to his body. His head, though still human, could definitely be called bear like in appearance. Without further conversation he started to moved towards me, raising his ax to take off my head as he did so.

"Oh, I didn't mean I was your bad day," I said as he came on. I then shouted "Miri!"

She'd been waiting for her cue. As if leaping over a hurtle my Daywalker lover leapt over both of our horses and landed with her father's sword cleaving downward. The bearshirt's head would have been split open like an overripe turnip if he hadn't leapt back at the last moment.

"She is," I said, as Miri not wanting to lose the momentum of her initial attack, moved forward with a series of figure eight attacks against the bearshirt.

I'll say this for the Titan follower he reacted quickly to the sudden role reversal. He gave ground as he either dodged or parried all of Miri's initial attacks.

While Miri kept their leader occupied, and therefore unable to issue orders, I started to finish off the other five Pagans. This had been our standard tactics when we were out numbered. I'd shock them all with a spell, Miri would take out the leader and I'd deal with the minions. As I brought up Lightning to send a bolt of electrical energy towards the Pagan that had the matchlock, I heard another gunpowder weapon discharge to my left. The back of the musketeer's head exploded as a 15mm lead ball entered and then exited it.

Sariel had joined the fight showing that the Fey were as skilled with modern firearms as they reputedly were with bows.

"I'll deal with the left, you deal with the right," she said as she drew her brace of horse pistols and started to circle away from me. The part of my head that was constantly curious about the world noted that Fey had to be a lot stronger than their appearance indicated because Sariel hefted the two heavy pistols that took the same powder and shot load as her carbine as if they were children's toys.

What my head focuses on while trying to track everything sometimes concerns me.

Turning to the remaining two Pagans, on my side of the fight I once again brought up Lightning channeled another bolt of electrical energy, that forked into both of them; putting the two back onto the ground that they had just risen from.

Checking upon Miri I saw that she had the situation well in hand. She had at one point cut the haft of the war ax into two pieces and the bearshirt was now trying to counter Miri superior speed and reach with a poorly balanced improvised weapon.

Miri, never one to toy with an opponent decided to end the fight once and for all. With an attack I've seen her use before, she pretended to thrust high right to draw the

Bearshirt's defences there. At the last moment she pivoted and spun counter clockwise. Using the full weight of her body to increase the attack's momentum she propelled a powerful swing to the low left cutting deep into the Bearshirt's calf. I felt a sudden surge of magic as the blade bit extra hard, breaking bone in what otherwise should have been a deep flesh wound. Miri followed up with a powerful kick to the bearshirt's stomach freeing the longsword's blade and causing a red spray of arterial blood to cover much of the ground beside him.

The kick also caused him to back step onto his now broken left leg which buckled causing him to go down onto one knee. Looking up the Bearshirt saw Miri standing before him, sword ready for a kill blow, eyes red and her fangs extended.

"What is it that you Old One worshipers say? 'The weak must survive on what the strong are willing to leave them.' Well survive on this!" she hissed.

Miri fully released her vampiric nature. Like a great forest cat, she was physically on him her fangs biting deep into the bear man's neck; sucking out his life's blood.

One leader down, first group of minions down, and looking past our particular fight, I saw that the villagers had taken advantage of our distraction to jump several of the Pagans and were starting their own revolt. Things were so far going to our way.

"ENOUGH!!"

The word erupted across the commons like a thunder clap from a clear blue sky: and everyone, (and I mean EVERYONE Miri, Sariel, me, every villager and every Pagan) turned to look at the speaker.

It was the leader of the intruders. Still standing upon the dais he had used a little of the Titan magic to quell the growing chaos that me and my friends had started. He used even more as he surrounded himself with a whirling firestorm which lifted him off the dais and propelled him towards me. Pagan and villager alike scrambled out of the way of the hot winds and flames.

Miri startled from her feeding by the Pagan's magic, seemed satisfied with the amount taken and appeared to 'calmly' run back to my side. Sariel as well was suddenly beside me, reloading one of her pistols as calmly as if she had been on Roland's practise field.

The Pagan leader cut the power to his spell and slowly sank to the ground about twenty-five metres from our where my friends and I stood. He was young for the position he seemed to hold. He looked to be in his mid-twenties, with a wild mane of dirty blonde hair and, given any other situation, a laughable attempt as a beard. Still his face was clear and his blue eyes, now roiling with anger, could if under the right circumstances could have cause hearts to skip a beat.

"How dare you disrupt the sacred ceremonies of your betters?" he asked; trying to project his voice as if we were across a battlefield, and not just a few metres away from each other.

I looked around at his down followers, most of whom were still lying on the ground, stunned. The exception was the bearshirt who was obviously using Pagan magic to both stop the bleeding and to heal the broken leg enough so that it could hold his weight.

Not letting this disturbing event raise any doubt in my head; I spun Lightning in my hand and released a bit of magic causing blue sparks to snap from the blade. Smiling I said, "I'll tell you when I meet my betters."

"Woman! How dare you address me in such a manner? It is clear to me that you're in desperate need of a firm hand to guide you back to your place. In the name of the First Gods I add you to this town's tribute. You will join the Titan Wald Stamm, and learn the joys of motherhood and..."

I didn't bother to learn what other joys I would

receive. Instead I threw a blast of focused wind which struck him low and hard in the stomach. The 'leader' went flying ten metres through the air and landed hard in the road between me and the larger crowd.

The infusion of the bearshirt's blood seemed to heighten Miri powers. She moved so fast that she appeared to teleport to where the bearshirt was slowing getting onto his feet testing the leg as he stood. Before he finished standing; Miri had the longsword's point touching his throat with just slightly less force than was needed to cut his skin.

"No. Just no," she said to the bearshirt with just a hint of a smile.

Sariel actually did teleport; ending up between us and another group of Pagans that were running towards their fallen leader. How someone who said that she couldn't cast spells kept preforming magic was beyond me.

Holding up both horse pistols steady at arm's length towards the advancing Pagans. "Now now boys let's allow our two leaders to finish their discussion," she said calmly cocking back the hammers.

This 'discussion' that I was having with their leader was not turning out to be as one sided as I had initially hoped for. The Druid had deflected much of my wind spell and while a bit battered, he wasn't as seriously hurt by it as I had hoped. Sitting up he cast one of his hands forward focusing his own magic into a spell aimed at me. I sensed the spell was acting upon the soil underneath my feet saturating it with water, quickly turning the soil into a mass of sticky mud.

In the split second before I started to sink into the morass I channeled my own magic into a spell whose dry warm winds lifted me off of the ground and flew me towards where the Pagan leader still lay. The winds tore my Tricorne hat from my head and my silver blonde hair flew out wildly around me.

Despite his spell failing to catch me, my opponent still had some tricks up his sleeve. I was hit with another spell which channeled magic directly into Thunder and Lightning causing the metal weapons to quickly heat up, becoming burning hot to the touch in a matter of seconds. With a cry of pain, I released the two stilettos from my now blistered hands. The shock of the pain and losing contact with my foci was enough to cause my loss of concentration on the spell, and I fell to the ground. Though I was able to roll as I landed, it still hurt and scrambled my thoughts enough I had to stay down on one knee as the Pagan bastard took control of the duel.

"Foolish girl! I've mastered control over the spirits of both air and land," shouted the Druid as he cast what I'm sure was supposed to be his finale.

Once again, the winds whipped up; only this time they weren't in my control, but in control of something else. Winds thrashed around me in a sphere perhaps two metres in diameter at first. The sphere soon started to decrease in radius increasing the strength and speed of the wind as it did so. The spherical tornado picked up dirt, grass and whatever else was on the ground making it appear as a solid living thing. By the time it was a metre across it started to suck out the air inside the of it.

It was not being able to breathe that actually managed to clear my head. I was going to die. Those women were going to be forced to produce children for men who they no desire to be with. Miri and possibly Sariel would try and stop them but outnumbered as they were they would die; or worst end up like those they were trying to save. And I was helpless to do a damn thing about it.

It was when I tried to look through the winds desperate to see my lover one last time that the magic kicked me out of my little pity party. It was then that I saw the truth of the Druid's words. Inside the whirling streams of air were dozens of tiny wind spirits; each controlling a piece of air, moving it with ever increasing speed. The Pagan leader in turn was controlling the wind spirits forcing them into this unnatural pattern. The same way I controlled the winds directly through my magic.

It was then that I got the idea of how I could beat this bastard. To do it though I'd have to channel magic in a way that only wild mages could do, and was the source of the stories of wild mages exploding for no reason.

I opened myself fully to the magic channeling more power than I ever have for any spell. As I took in the magic I felt my body rebel against the power, blood vessels burst, bones cracked, and an airless scream escaped my mouth as it felt like my entire body was suddenly on fire.

But I kept control of the magic forcing it into my hands until both were pulsing with raw magical energy. Only when I couldn't take the pain anymore did I shove them both into the wind sphere and released the magic. I felt the wind spirits die as the magic first overwhelmed them and then forced them into the actual wind streams themselves. The magic flowed through me at such a rate that it felt as if another being was trying to possess me. How could any mortal, especially one so small and young control it? Using me as a conduit and the winds as a weapon, the magic wanted nothing less than to tear the entire world apart.

Only I wouldn't let it. With every gram of strength that I had left I stood up and directed the magic into the pattern that I had chosen for it. This little girl was able to control the power that she had unleashed and she was able to bend it to her will. The magic screamed in protest. But those screams were lost in the howls of the winds, as I turned the sphere into a circle open at the top so that I could breathe in the cool fall air. Standing in the eye of my personal tornado, I had the space and time to invoke the last part of my attack. Increasing the wind's speed even more, it dried out the air so much, that static electricity started to crackle through the dust.

Looking over towards the Druid I saw that he didn't look at all scared. Instead he looked confused. He was shouting, trying to command wind spirits that were no longer there, all in an doomed attempt to regain control of the storm.

"You idiot! You think because you can force air spirits into making a storm that makes you special. I am the wind; I am the STORM!" I shouted as I redirected the wind one final time. I felt the ribs on the right side of my body crack and then break as I forced my tornado into a one metre funnel directly towards the druid.

The bastard didn't even try and move; convinced he was still in control of the situation right up to the time that the wind, dust, and dry lightning removed his physical body from existence. I had managed somehow to think ahead and forced the funnel of my tornado upwards. The winds passing harmlessly, over the villager's and Pagan's heads: up into the air to dissipate a hundred metres above us. The clouds were forced to part, and the rays of the mid-morning sun broke through; promising good things for the rest of the day.

Only once the winds had settled down did I close myself to the magic. Barely able to stand, I was about to start moving towards the bearshirt when my tricorne landed in front of me: a bit battered but otherwise in perfect shape.

With great effort I leaned over and not only managed to pick up the hat, but I stayed standing as well. It was a bit difficult to walk the first few steps to my destination by I was determined to see this finished.

Miri was still holding her sword to the bearshirt's throat, but neither of them was really noticing it anymore. Both shared a look of unbelief on their faces.

Finally understanding why book mages always seem to walk with a staff in hand, I tried desperately not to sway as I said to the bearshirt, "This is what is going to happen next. You and the rest of your men are going to leave this village, and you're leaving all the women here. You're never going to take another girl from this village or any other. If you do: I will know. For I am the storm: I am one with every raindrop, every dark cloud, and every breeze. Take one woman against her will and I will make today look like a gentle summer breeze. Understand me?"

Okay that was all pure bullshit, but he didn't know that. Besides, given the spell I had just cast; right at that moment I felt like I could have made good on that threat. At least I did until the guy started laughing. And I don't mean a short chuckle I mean a genuine belly laugh so full of good humour it was almost contagious.

As he continued to laugh, he looked up at Miri, then down at her longsword; his expression, wordlessly asking if she'd mind terrible removing the tip from his throat. Miri having just fed and therefore in a generally positive mood did so with an apologetic shrug of her shoulders.

The large man then got up to his full height. Only when he directly faced me did he stop laughing; though the mirth was still clear on his face as he said "No, you can't girl. You're not the first wild mage I've faced and while I've never seen any other of your kind let in the spirit of the storm like that; you're not that powerful."

"Have no fear girl it shall be as you say," he said holding up a hand so he could continue to speak. "You've got balls girl and that should be respected. Besides that, young buck could have used the blessings that the Old Ones gave him to help ease our children into this world and keep our women folk safe during their birthings. Instead he thought only of power and control."

Turning the bearshirt looked around for his ax head. Seeing it, he picked it up and started to leave. After several steps he turned back to me and asked with genuine curiosity. "Just what was your business in the village in the first place?"

Thinking only clearly enough to say the truth I said; "we're part of a mercenary company hired by the Prince of Ulm to battle the Titan Spawn that are threatening his lands. I just came to this village to let them know we were passing through."

He took that in for a bit and then said "A good cause, I hope you have a worthy fight." Turning he started to walk toward his men again and shouted "Right my friends, we're heading home. You're just going to have to settle for the wives you already have."

I watched them go. Both Miri and Sariel came to stand beside me with a mixture of both fear and concern on their faces,

Don't worry, I'm fine, I managed to get out before slumping to Miri's arms a comfortable blackness enveloping me as I did so.

Chapter 2

I awoke in a bed; which given that I'd been sleeping on the ground for two weeks was a pleasant surprise. Slowly I started to move my limbs. I was shocked that I felt as little pain as I did; though it did feel like I was swathed head to foot in bandages. Looking at my left arm I saw that it was tied down and one of Keira's healing infusions was intravenously entering my system.

"She's awake," I heard Miri say as I felt her take my right hand into hers. Squeezing it gently and she said. "Hey you; how are you feeling?"

"Not bad actually," I replied as I started to rise.

Fresh pain shot through my right hand as Miri's squeeze suddenly felt like a steel vice. "Not bad, NOT BAD! You stupid bitch! You nearly blow yourself up and you say that you're feeling 'not bad'. Oh, when you get out of this bed I'm so going to put you right back into it and not in a good way!"

"Miri! You lost the toss, no jumping the queue. Go and let Keira know that Sasha is awake," Riley said as he flapped down from a rafter to land on my chest.

With a dramatically loud sigh, Miri let go of my hand and started to head to the door, but not before reaching forward and kissing me hard on the lips. "I'm not done yelling at you," she said before leaving the room.

Before I could ask Riley about the queue he was talking about the Raven gave me a hard peck right between my eyes.

"Riley!" I gasped in surprise.

"Don't you 'Riley' me young lady. I know you're a wild mage but really, I thought we were passed you being a complete idiot. What were you thinking? No strike that, when did you stop thinking?"

"I thought that I was going to die, and that people I cared for were also going to die. And then I saw an opportunity to turn things around and I took it," I said somewhat angry. I was alive; everyone else was safe. So why was everyone so pissed at me?

"So, to avoid dying you tried your hand at spontaneous spell casting?" he asked. Riley hadn't been this exasperated with me since I first started to learn to control my magic.

I think he was going to say something more but his foot slipped on one of my bandages and his weight fell upon an area of my chest where the bones were still knitting together. Sudden pain shot through me as I cramped up in response. That I was in intense pain caused Riley to lose a lot of his anger with me. He flapped over to his usual position near one of my shoulders.

Once there he let out his own big sigh and said, as if reading my mind, "The reason why everyone is so mad at you is because you gave us a really good scare. First by nearly dying; and then by trying to control raw magic. You know what happens to most wild mages that try to access the magic like that? They explode and take everyone around with them. That you're still alive means that you must have eaten a horse shoe this morning with the amount of luck that you've shown."

"Or that you taught me really well," I said trying to suck up to my familiar.

That got me a nip on the ear. "Don't you dare ask why you deserved that. And count yourself lucky if you had said something about 'being that good', I would have taken your entire ear off," Riley said being entirely honest.

I reached up with my untied hand and stroked the soft feathers under his chin, "I'm sorry," I said to him.

Riley sighed again and then chuckled. Returning the affectionate gesture, he rubbed my chin and cheek with his head.

"Don't do that again," He said in a tone that made me feel like everything was going to be okay.

Then a stray thought floated into my head about

99

something that Riley had said earlier.

"Riley?" I started.

"Yes?" he responded.

"What toss?" I asked.

He chuckled a bit and then said, "Oh there are a number of people who are quite cross with you right now. Keira insisted that we draw lots to see who got to yell at first; I won."

I think I was better off in the Druid's tornado.

Chapter 3

Riley and I didn't talk for the next few minutes, just enjoying the silence together. Then the door opened again and Keira of Quellwasser and Miri once again entered the room. The Book Mage's eyes were wide and dilated, showing that she had opened her mage sight before entering the room. Moving over to the left side of my bed she replaced her intravenous healing concoction with another lighter in colour solution.

Related to her interest in mechanical life, the book mage had a keen interest in the magic to heal mortal. I've been told by others that while she's not as capable as the clerics of the betrayer Gods, her infusions and healing potions are still far more effective than what other mages have been able to do.

Miri looked towards Keira and then Riley and asked, "So is she well enough for me to yell at her yet?"

"Let see," said Keira as she thumped my rib cage right where Riley had stepped.

I croaked in pain and tried to curl up into a ball again. Keira appeared not to notice and proceeded to first check both my hands then threw back my blankets. Looking down I saw that I really was wrapped from the neck down in bandages. She removed the outer wraps from around my hips. These were followed by the dressings that had covered the scars I first received when that lightning bolt had transformed me into a wild mage. I noted with concern that while the outer bandages were reasonably clean the actual dressings were soiled with what appeared to be blood and other bodily fluids.

Once the bandages were removed, she reached under the bed and produced a ceramic chamber pot. "Arch your back please," she ordered.

Without really thinking about it I did as I was told. Then Keira slid the chamber pot under me. After a few

101

seconds she asked, "You don't have to go?"

Actually, I did, but before I could say anything she moved to the head of the bed and rearranged my pillows so that I was in a sitting position. "Sorry should have thought of that. There you go," Keira said triumphantly as if that was the problem.

When I still didn't start to relieve myself the book mage's complexion once again turned concern, "Are you unable to go?" she asked her voice growing a bit alarmed.

"I think I could: but I usually don't have an audience when I do so?" I replied.

"Why would that make a difference?" Keira asked genuinely confused.

Miri, who by this time was openly laughing at my discomfort, moved over to Keira, and gently took her by the arm.

"She's very shy about these things, you know Dwarven upbringing and all," my lover explained to the Book Mage.

"Really, I hadn't realized that Dwarfs had taboos against public urination," said Keira completely missing the fact that Mimi was joking.

As they were leaving I turned my head towards Riley.

"Well," I said.

"What? It's not like this is the first time, remember when you were in that tickle fight with Julian and you were laughing too hard," he started.

"Out," I said with enough force that I hurt my ribs again and ended up grimacing in pain.

"Alright, alright I'll go," he said flapping his wings and landing on Miri's shoulder.

Once I was finally alone I lay back and tried to relax. Both so I could take a piss but as well to try to make sense of the recent events.

There was a knock at the door and Keira stuck her head into the room again and said "If you could also provide a stool sample as well that would really be helpful."

On reflex I sent out a small bolt of lightning towards Keria's head. The bolt was extremely weak and ended up being nothing more than a large spark that barely got two feet from me. It had enough power however to cause my entire body to seize up in pain.

Seeing me cast a spell Keira had wisely ducked her head out of the room, but she quickly looked back in, and said perfectly straight faced. "I would avoid using magic for the next few days. You overloaded your system and your body can't channel the energies right now."

She closed the door again but not before I could hear both Miri and Riley laughing loudly outside the door.

Chapter 4

After fulfilling my duties as Keira's patient, she went off to examine the evidence while Miri removed the remainder of my bandages and got me dressed in a large man's shirt that had to be draped over my left side due to the arm still being tied down. After I was clothed, Miri fed me some fresh chicken vegetable broth. Having something in my stomach made me realise just how hungry I was and I definitely wanted more to eat. But I also definitely wanted to know when I could get out of this bed. I'm normally very active and I have a problem staying in bed even one that I'm not sharing with anyone. I was in the middle of trying to get Miri and Riley to let me up when Keira re-entered the room.

"Ah you're still in bed; good. Miri does appear to make an excellent nurse. I have a full list of your conditions to share with you," she said in that matter of fact tone she sometimes gets when she's in the middle of analysing things.

"During your dual with the Pagan druid you suffered:

three broken ribs; numerous burst blood vessels throughout your body; your scar tissue started to discharge blood and salt water; your hands look like they were in a desert wind storm for a week, while your palms are badly blistered from burns, and you've lost three finger nails.

"The good news is that your urine and stool samples show no blood in your digestive system so no internal damage. This along with the two healing infusions that I've introduced directly into your system means you should be able to get up from that bed in a day or two. More than enough time for you to catch up with the rest of the Company as we make our way through the Titan Wald.

As she listed my injuries I was glad to be alive. I was also beginning to understand how close my attempts at creating and casting a spell at the same time had been to killing me.

"Shit Keira just how much magic did she channel?" Miri asked a bit awed.

"As you know; mages have never been able to agree on an exact unit of measurement for magical energy. The best answer I can give you, other than 'a lot', is that based upon my examination of the place where she cast the spell. From the measurement that I took I'd say that she channeled a comparable amount to what other wild mages were channelling right before they exploded.

"Seriously Sasha if you had lost control of that much magic half the town would have been destroyed," said Keira her voice even and matter of fact.

"Now you understand why I was so pissed at you," said Riley.

"I felt the magic wanting to be free and to destroy, when I was casting the spell. It felt so pissed that I kept it under control," I replied.

"You make it sound like magic is a living thing," said Miri.

"In large enough volumes, magic mirrors the inner

104

emotions of the caster. Given that you were in a fight for your life, it's not surprising that you interpreted the magic that way," said Keira quietly. It appeared that I'd managed to impress the book mage. "But that's enough magic theory for one day. Right now Sasha needs to sleep so that her body can focus on healing."

Miri moved over and pulled the pillows out from under me so that I was lying flat on the bed again. She then leaned over and gave me one more kiss and then took the tray my soup came on and walked out.

"Keira is right stay in bed and rest. You're going to need all of your strength with what's going to happen now," Riley said somewhat cryptically as he flew back up to his normal position in the room's rafters.

I pondered that thought for several seconds before sleep overcame me.
　　　**

The next day I received several more visitors, including the village mayor and Sariel. The Fey didn't stay that long as she appeared to be afraid of me all of a sudden. Maybe wild mages blew up more often in the Fey Reich.

The last person to see me that day was Roland. That Miri, Sariel and I had accomplished Roland's basic orders still didn't stop him from being one of the people that wanted to yell at me. Fortunately for me by the time it was his turn he had calmed down enough that he just talked at his normal volume. After the usual inquiries as to how I was feeling, Roland asked Miri and Riley to leave us alone. Once they left as he usually did Roland got right to the point.

"I'm docking you three days pay. I was tempted to dock Miri and Sariel as well, but technically you were in command and therefore responsible for this catastrophe.

"Catastrophe?" I asked incredulously. "As far as I can tell the villagers welcomed the Company with open arms and are bending over backwards to help us in anyway they can."

"Yes, we'll get to the results of your stunt later, right now let's talk about the stunt itself. When I hired you and your friends it was because of your proven experience as independent scouts and your skills in arcane matters. It wasn't so you could go off half-cocked as big ass heroes. When you saw what was happening in town you should have pulled back observed and gotten word back to me so that I could have made the call as commanding officer. Instead you let your emotions get the better of you and you ran into a situation alone without back up."

"I sent Riley," I said trying to defend my actions.

"Yes, as an afterthought, while you three started a fight where you were outnumbered ten to one," Roland countered.

"They could have been ending and getting ready to leave," I pointed out.

"Or they might have been there for the rest of the day," Roland countered. "The point being that we'll never know because you didn't. Instead you went in half cocked, and yes before you say anything you did 'win', but at a high cost."

I glared at the two and a half metre tall Golem, the description whiny little bitch didn't fit physically but right then it sure was the description I wanted to put on his behavior.

While he was impossible to read, Roland did have knack for reading others. "Oh I'm not talking about your minor injuries. Keira's infusions have taken care of those. I'm talking about the real cost."

He leaned back, saying more to himself than me, "How to say this so that it gets through that thick head of yours," then getting a starting place he leaned forward again. "Do you know where you are?"

I mouth went off before I could think. "Letzte Moglichkeit," I said.

106

Roland chose to ignore my snark "You're in the mayor's house, in fact you're in the mayor's bed. And do you know why you're here?"

"I would guess that one of the chosen girls was his daughter, and he was grateful," I replied.

"Granddaughter, and in part you were correct I will give you that. However, the reason why you're here, the reason why the rest of the Company was offered virtually anything they wanted for free, is because your little stunt scared them shitless and they're afraid of us," he said: and for the first time ever I could hear emotion in his normally monotone voice.

"The Reichs are full of fear Sasha, and with the breach of the covenant they have no good choices to turn to with that fear. So, it festers and grows until they feel it is hopeless and they do something foolish. Like looking to the Phoenix Republic, or a Demon for answers," he started.

"But I'm as mortal as any of them," I started.

"Are you? You tore your opponent to shreds through a display of will that even caused Keira to pale when she saw the aftermath. You may be mortal, but how reassuring is the explanation 'Oh I took control of a tornado and used it to tear my opponent apart. Anyone who was struck by lightning and survived could have done that'?"

For once my brain clamped down on my mouth long enough for me to realize that Roland had a point. More than a point he was right; damn him.

"It's not very reassuring," I said weakly.

"You're damn right it isn't. Sasha you're a wild mage, you didn't ask for these powers I know. But you have them, and that means that you have responsibility to use them for the betterment of your fellow mortals, just like Keira and myself."

I felt tears starting to fill my eyes, one of my Dwarf aunts gave me a similar talk a couple of years ago when I'd first gotten control of these powers. But I was so full with

107

wonder at the time it had gone in one ear and out the other. This time the words were staying and I started to feel the full weight of their meaning.

I think Roland saw that his words were a having an effect, because his tone softened a bit. "Part of this is my fault. I employ a lot of hero types; there are so many more soldants now a days than before. Normally when I do, I have a long sit down with them and explain what I expect from them. I didn't with you and Miri because of our past experience. And I see that was a mistake now so here it goes. I expect two things from the extraordinary people I employ. First, I expect you to help reduce the fear in this world, to give people hope. The second is to stay alive. The best way to accomplish both is to work as part of a team. Understand?"

I nodded the tears starting to flow openly. Suddenly Roland reached forward and gave me a hug. Believe it or not being hugged by two hundred kilos of steel, wood and leather actually does help. I laughed and said "Do you give hugs to all the sellswords in your employ?"

"Oh yes, you'd be surprise with how effective giving a hug to a hobgoblin can be," Roland said, back to his completely deadpan tone.

I couldn't help it, I started to laugh again as my commanding officer left me with a better understanding of why the whys of my actions were just as important as the hows.

The Company

Chapter 1

The next day Roland and the Company headed north on the Old Empire road towards Ulm. Sariel went with them, the Fey was getting bored with Letzte Moglichkeit and a bored Fey was never a good thing. The fact that it appeared that the Fey may have become a little afraid of me, might have added to her desire to live. She had never seen a human wield significant magical power before this, and the thought that mortals, other than the Fey, could do so might have caused a crisis of faith.

So that left Miri, Riley and I in the village. Despite how much I enjoyed the mayor's bed, I decided to move into one of the three inns in Letzte Moglichkeit for the remainder of my recovery. I was surprised that a village this size had three inns but I guess with this being the last village on this side of the Wald, it just saw that much traffic.

Roland had paid room and board in all of the rooms in the inn for a week, so I just moved into the nicest one as Keira and Sariel moved out. Not having to pay anything gave Miri and I a break on our now reduced purse which I hoped indicated a change in our luck. It was a nice enough room; there weren't any bedbugs in the mattress or a nightmare in the closet, which were always a plus. I was feeling a lot better by then as well. Most of the bruises had faded and the broken ribs while still tender, no longer caused me to curl up into a ball when they were touched. I tired easily though and any magic I tried to cast took too much effort to justify the result.

But I was healing. My improved state of being was enough for a still randy Miri, who was still in a post feeding high; 'suggested' that we engage in a bout of 'gentle' loved making. Well several bouts in fact, as we stayed in the village for two more days.

Finally on the evening of the second day after the Company had left; I decided that I had enough bed rest, and it was time to get up and get moving. The next dawn, I set about quietly packing while Miri slept. For a badass sellsword and Daywalker daughter of an ancient Vampire, Miri was actually a very sound sleeper. So by the time she had finally awakened I had washed, dressed and packed both of our belongings.

"I take it you feel better?" she asked as she rolled over to look at me.

"Bored out of my skull more like, you spend four days in bed where the only things you're allowed to do are eat, sleep and screw and you'd be climbing the walls to," I replied.

"So you find my love making boring," said Miri with a dangerous lilt to her voice.

"Can we hold off on parsing each of my words and how they make you feel until we are actually on the road? It will give us something to talk about, and we can have makeup sex by firelight tonight," I replied trying desperately to keep us moving towards leaving.

Miri considered that and then got up used the chamber pot, had an amazingly quick bird bath and was mostly dressed by the time I'd gotten our breakfast of day old rye bread, hard cheese and a pot of ale from where the innkeeper had laid it out for me the night before.

As we ate, Riley tapped at the window to be let in.

"I take it you're feeling well enough to travel?" he asked when I let him in.

"More like too bored to stay in bed another day," I said.

"Different side of the same coin," he said came down and swiped a piece of cheese from my plate. After he managed to swallow the piece hole he said "By the way there's a surprise down stairs for you."

111

As a child a 'surprise' usually meant a lovingly crafted Dwarven dessert, or even a handmade doll, and I loved them dearly. Riley's definition of 'surprise' was often a lot darker than those childhood memories and I no longer got 'excited' about surprises.

"What sort of surprise?" Miri asked being a lot braver than me.

"Come down and see. It's not a bad thing: well I don't think it's a bad thing. Anyways come on down and see," Riley said with growing excitement.

Now I was just plain curious. Riley getting excited about something wasn't an everyday occurrence, so I headed downstairs to see what had gotten him so flustered. The common area of the Inn was empty with Miri and I being the only guests not even the innkeeper had bother to get up yet. Exiting the building I saw what Riley had been talking about, and I'll give the Raven his due, I was surprised.

There leaning against the Inn's wall, sleeping soundly, was the bearshirt that Miri had beaten less than a week earlier. Next to his right hand was his ax; its new haft I noted was reinforced with thin steel strips. Circled around his left hand were the reins of a pair of shaggy northern mules, one with a saddle and the other loaded down with a season's worth of supplies.

As if the pressure of our stare was enough the bearshirt snorted awake and looked around. When his eyes finally focused on me his face broke out in a wide smile.

"Ah the storm mage good good, are we ready to leave?" he said directly to me.

I admit that I was very (no Dwarf understatement here) taken aback by his statement and I didn't know how to respond.

Fortunately Miri did, "We? As in you and us: together?" she asked in a tone that made it clear that she wasn't entirely sure what was going on either.

"Why yes I mean us together. Has the word 'we' changed meaning recently?" he replied now equally confused.

Well at least we were now all experiencing the same emotion.

"Alright let's start this from the top. Just to cover bases; you are the same bearshirt whose leader I tore into little pieces last week correct?" I asked trying to get my bearings.

"Yes I am the same bearshirt; my name is Gregor Waldjager," he replied.

"We'll get to names in a second," I said cutting him off. "And you know that we're heading north on a contract to fight Titan Spawn?"

"Yes. That is why I am coming with you," Gregor started again.

I held up my hand to get him to stop talking again, still trying to get everything connected in my brain. I looked at Miri and was somewhat relieved to see that she was confused as I was.

"But you worship the Old Ones. More than that you get powers from them: why do you want to come with us to fight them?" I said to him still confused.

There was a good 10 seconds of silence before he asked a little exasperated "Can I talk now?"

My cheeks turned red, I had been rude to him but I mean he and Miri were trying to kill each other last week so it wasn't like I didn't have a reason. Still I felt it necessary to say "I'm sorry, I was being rude, please go ahead."

"As I said; my name is Gregor Waldjager. I am, as you call me, a bearshirt and I am coming North with you to fight the Titan Spawn. I do so first because they worship the Titans not the Old Ones," he started then stopped holding up his hand this time to stop me from asking "but aren't they the same thing?"

113

"Before you ask; no The Old Ones are different from Titans. Old Ones gift their followers with powers. Titans only take; they never give," he said firmly. We Pagans have been fighting the Spawn long before the Dying rebalanced the world, but that is only part of why I am coming with you," he said finally.

"Okay what are the other reasons?" I asked.

"Oh this should be good," whispered Riley into my ear.

"I like you girl, you're interesting and you should provide me with a lot of opportunities to fight. Your girlfriend beat me too easily. All that living in one spot, with enough food to eat and women to screw has made me soft. I need to get out into the world to get my edge back," he said as he ticked the reason off on his large fingers.

"Oh that was better than I hoped. Can we keep him? The entertainment value alone is worth having him along," Riley said into my ear.

"OOKay let's see if I got this straight; because Miri beat you in a fight, and you think I'm interesting," I started.

"I think he means that you attract trouble like shit attracts flies," interrupted Riley.

"Yes your talking bird has it correct. You are very smart even compared to other Ravens," Gregor said to Riley.

"Oh that tears it; he's hired," said Riley.

"You just want him around because you won't be the lone male in a group of women," said Miri.

"Hey! That's another reason. Gregor what's your opinion on eyeballs," Riley asked excitedly.

"To eat? I can take them or leave them," he said casually.

"Good enough, equal share of all found plunder and you have to pay for any extra room and bored resulting from not sharing a room with the ladies," said Riley as an opening statement of negotiation.

114

"Riley!" I said crossly.

"What? I making sure that he's not expecting to sleep with either of you?" replied the Raven.

"That's not the point," I started to say.

"Though a good boundary that we should have set for Sariel, she seemed a little too expectant in the Taleless Rat," said Miri.

"Your companion with the flintlocks? I'd not say no if she offered," replied Gregor.

"Sleeping with a Fey is like sleeping with crazy, it might be fun at the time but it will always end up biting you in the ass," replied Miri with a tone that made it clear that she had been speaking from experience.

"How do you know about sleeping with either?" I started to ask Miri without any jealousy whatsoever, then realizing that I'd lost complete control of the conversation, I changed tacks.

"The point that I'm trying to make is that less than a week ago we were trying to kill each other and now you want to join forces. Am I the only one who finds this more than a little strange?" I said to everyone, trying to regain my original point in this strange discussion.

"No, it's only a little strange for this day and age. Sasha; right now, you've got the biggest balls in region and that tends to attract people. I say; let's take him with us and see what Roland says about hiring him," replied Miri, she then added, "Though Riley's stipulations are still in force."

"I can live with that," replied Gregor as he looked me up and down curiosity on his face.

"Balls as a figure of speech, she's completely a woman," explained Riley.

"Oh. Now I get it," said the bearshirt.

"Okay he's coming with us until Roland can have his say. Now if you excuse me I need to finish packing so we can get out of here before noon," I said desperately wanting to get something stronger than ale to drink regardless of the

115

time of day.

Chapter 2

Our first day riding was hard for me. It felt like I'd been on campaign for months not resting in a soft bed for a week. While that was mostly me still healing, the environment also played a part. The road through the Wald was in a word; depressing. It wasn't the fact that the trees grew right up to the sides of the road. Instead it was the fact that they actually grew over the Old Empire road and in a consistent arch the was close to four meters high at its apex, and it stayed like that kilometre after kilometre that really creeped me out.

"It's like being in a living tunnel," I said aloud, then turning to Gregor I asked, "Is it like this the whole way?"

The bearshirt kicked his mule up to ride next to me before he answered, "Pretty much, sometimes a large rock or small rise of stone prevents the trees from growing but where it is clear yes, it is like this. The Deer Track is a strange place even by Pagan standards,"

"Deer Track?" I asked.

"What else would you call it? All you city dwellers take the road to move through the forest like a deer uses their favorite track. So when we want to get tribute, all we had to do was to wait in ambush along the road. No need to look for you city dwellers, you always come the same way," Gregor explained.

"Makes sense," said Miri. "Not saying I like the idea, but it does make sense," she added when she saw my disapproving look.

I didn't say a word to either of them for an hour.

While it was like one large tunnel it was still an intact Old Empire road and we made good time along it solid flat surface. As midday turned into evening, and it started to get dark in the tunnel, we began to come upon some of the 'improvised' camp spots along the sides of the road. The ones that travellers had felled the trees and cut back the brush still existed, but new growth had clogged the space. In what must have been an ogre campsite a large rock had been smashed smooth on the top and large handholds had been carved into the rock's side.

Miri, still somewhat 'up' from her feeding, couldn't help but impulsively investigate. Leaping off of her horse she climbed the handholds to the top rock that was actually above the lower canopy. Disappearing from view we heard an uncharacteristic squeal of delight from the Daywalker.

"Sasha you have to come up here. It's like your own little secret world. The ogres even chopped out a bit of a chimney to vent away the smoke from their cooking fires," she said still on the top.

"Well now she's got me curious," said Riley as he flew up to take a look around.

I sighed knowing that once again I was going to be the voice of reason. "Guys we can't use that camp. There is no way that we can get the horses up there and they're too vulnerable to leave them alone this near the road.

"Are you sure, Sasha? Miri's right this place is pretty cool. You'd not even have to pitch a tent up here; the branches are so woven together that its bone dry.

I gave Gregor a frustrated look which he returned with a nonplussed 'kids these days' shrug and I shouted back, "Yes I'm sure, now both of you get back down here so we can find a place to camp before we lose all the light."

Both of my closest friends came back down, sulking. I should have felt bad, but I was too tired from the day's ride to care at that point. Finally, we found another campsite not too far along that could accommodate us and our mounts. As was the case with the road, the canopy over the camping area was thick enough that we didn't bother pitching the tent; instead we just took care of the horses got a fire going and heated up the smoked ham we'd been given as a parting gift from the village along with some toasted bread for dinner.

Gregor had turned out to be an enjoyable traveling companion, he chipped in setting up camp without question and his sharp cheese was delicious melted over the ham and toast. I was just nicely settling down for the night when the howling started.

Gregor was first to jolt upright upon hearing the noise. Miri wasn't too far behind; drawing her longsword as she rose to stand in the centre of the clearing.

"Gnolls," said Gregor making the word sound more like a curse than a name.

Gnolls were a particularly vicious type of Titan Spawn. They were thoroughly and irredeemably corrupted by Titan magic; blending the best parts of a wolf or dog with the worst parts of a mortal into a single being. Ranging between two and a half and three metres in height, these fur covered, wolf headed creatures were blood thirsty mortals that attacked using the tactics and structure of wolf pack, a nasty combination at the best of times. In the claustrophobic Titan Wald there was a good chance we'd not be walking out of here.

As the Daywalker and bearshirt looked out into the gloom of the woods around us, I grabbed the reins of our animals and moved them into the centre of the clearing as well. Our horses were old campaigners and had seen enough unnatural things not to be scared easily; while Gregor's mules were so calm, they appeared to be more pissed at me for interrupting their dinner than they were by the upcoming Gnoll attack.

"They'll attack from the road, the forest is too thick for them to charge from," hissed Gregor, as he hefted his repaired ax in his hands.

"Let's make sure of that," I said pulling out my two stiletto foci. I figured that this would be a test of how useful my magic was going to be in the fight. Pointing Lightning at the forest's edge I channelled the magic through its length and sent out a curtain of lightning out into the thick mat of dead leaves and branches. It took several seconds but soon numerous small fires were burning around the camp. Bringing up Thunder I caused a warm dry breeze to form, feeding the fires of the winter damp fuel and causing them to join together into several large self-sustaining fires that secured, at least from the Gnolls, the forest side of our encampment.

Once I was done I was breathing hard and the sweat that I had broken into had nothing to do with the heat the fires were generating. What I had done wasn't the most challenging of my spells, but still I'd felt it. On the positive side, I cast the spells effectively and I was still standing without backlash.

"Sasha, don't spend all of your power on theatrics! We're going to need you when we attack," warned Miri.

"Nice to have a warm fight though; I hate fighting in the cold," quipped Gregor. As he did so, I could feel him starting to draw upon his Pagan magic. Within seconds the physical manifestations of the magic started to appear, as his body hair became thicker, his already burly build becoming even burlier; and well bear like.

I sure Riley was going to give his opinion regarding my magic use, but it was right about that time that the Gnolls came into view.

There was half a dozen of the creatures. All were dressed in poorly maintained jerkins of metal reinforced leather which hung loosely over their matted and mangy body fur. Most were armed with large jagged slabs of gore spattered metal that were supposed to be axes or spears and large shields made of thick planks of green timber. However, the largest and I imagined the leader, was armed with a massive two-handed club that wasn't anything more than a two-metre tree bound in strips of metal with several large metal spikes driven through the business end. A crude weapon: but one that would break every bone in my body, if I was struck by it.

"Paaagannnn I see you have two breeders. Give them too usss and you can go on yourrr way," said the Leader as he leered at both Miri and I. Most types of Titan Spawn are always male; they increase their numbers in only two ways. The first is for a Titan to play with more mortals; transforming them into Spawn. The other is for the Spawn to 'mate' with a mortal female. In the case of the Gnolls the pregnancy is mercifully short, only three months on average. The pregnancy ends when the litter of four to six Gnolls tears themselves out of the mother's abdomen. Its considered a good sign if the mother lives through the birthing so that the litter can devour her still beating heart as a sign of brotherly unity.

Needless to say, few mortals; male or female, tolerate Spawn of any sort and Gnolls are near universally loathed.

Gregor was wonderfully normal in this regard. Instead of carrying on the banter Gregor just roared at the Gnolls. Charging the closest one, he cleaved through its shield and deep into the monster's arm. Then with an even greater display of strength the bearshirt wrenched free his ax from both shield and arm, sending arterial blood spraying up into the tree branches above.

As he did so, I cast the same wind spell that I used just over a week before on Gregor's men. The tornado strong winds blasted over the Gnoll's leader and his surrounding followers. The lessor Gnolls were blown from their feet. The leader braced his tree branch upon the ground and managed to stay upright. Not the best outcome I could have had but at least he was in no position to defend himself when Miri, following our usual tactic, charged in; her longsword already aimed at the Leader's head.

The large Gnoll had no choice but to let go of his tree branch and leap to one side. His timing was nearly perfect and he only lost his left wolf like ear and several centimetres of scalp to Miri's magical blade.

"Bitch youuuu will pay for that," he said as he kicked

121

out at the Daywalker with his reverse jointed leg, catching Miri square in the stomach. The blow sent Miri back two meters but she managed to keep her feet as well. A second later she was back engaging the Leader in a one on one fight.

My job of course, was to keep that fight one on one, so that Miri could take out the leader as quickly as possible. That my lover might lose against such a monster never entered my mind. With Gregor keeping two busy, that left me with three Gnolls who were intelligent enough to follow the basic tactical doctrine of modern combat.

Kill the Mage first.

Fortunately, I was hard to kill quickly; and the last thing you wanted to do with a Wild Mage (well any Mage really) was to give them time.

The Gnoll's first mistake was thinking that they could hem me into some sort of corner where I couldn't dodge their attacks. They approach me shields up, forming an impenetrable line of flesh and wood.

Or at least that's what they thought. I waited until they were close and then cast a spell that I had mastered just before the Company started our march to Ulm. As I backed away, I funneled the magic through the tip of lightning instead of the hilt and pulled it into my body. I released the magic and it transformed me from living flesh into a bolt of living lightning. I then ran (for lack of a better word) through the three of them leaving each of the monsters with two large and very painful burns where I had entered and then left their bodies. Once I'd moved through all of them, I reformed the lightning into my mortal body some four metres behind them.

I could tell the three of them were confused by the frantic shifting of their heads back and forth trying to figure out where I was. The smart one of the three had just started to turn around when I let loose with a thunderous windblast which sounded even louder than usual given the close

122

confines of the hard wood forest.

All three of the Gnolls reacted as if they'd been struck by the blast of wind, even though none of them had been the target. Only after several confused seconds had past did they realized that none of them had been the hit. Finally, they turned around to see where I was.

That confusion saved me a lot of embarrassment. You see I had aimed the wind blast directly upwards into the forest canopy. Unfortunately, this meant that all the leaves, sticks and several large branches that had been part of the canopy came crashing down around and onto me. One particularly large branch clipped my shoulder hard enough that I was sure it was going to bruise. But that was a necessary price to pay, given what I was going to do next.

Now that they knew where I was, the three Gnolls moved as one; charging me, their cleaver shaped weapons swinging as they came.

But I was ready, and just as they were about to hit me, I released my most powerful spell (well second most powerful but I didn't even want to consider casting that other spell again for a good long time).

The spell started with another loud clap of thunder only this time it was directly under me. The blast was powerful enough to both stop the three Gnolls in their tracks and propel me up into the air. I can direct where the spell sends me as if I was shot from a howitzer. But this time I sent myself straight up into the air. This was why I sent the wind blast upwards; to clear a path for me to follow. Even with the previous wind blast I felt several small branches scrape across my face and hands. As I started to come down, the spell accelerated my speed and I landed with another loud explosion that sent the big monster's flying to the ground the fight knocked out of them as sure as their wind was.

Not wanting to waste the time I'd just bought for myself. I rushed forward to one of the stunned Gnolls and

123

drove Lightning through its side close to his heart. The bolt of lightning I then channeled deep into the Gnoll's body exploding the creature's heart while it cooked its other organs.

Turning to the other two Gnolls, I saw that my companions having finished their personal fights were already taking care of them.

And suddenly the forest was quiet again; with only the sound of Miri, Gregor and my breathing being heard.

As the heat of battle left me, I suddenly felt very tired and collapsed onto the ground.

"And I thought my second wife was loud," said Gregor breaking the silence.

"You haven't heard anything; she's a screamer in bed," replied Miri as she cleaned her longsword.

"I'd suggest we stop worrying about that and grab our things and get out of here. If there are any other Gnoll packs out there they'll know where to find us," I said wanting desperately to change the subject.

"Oh, and whose fault is that," said Miri moving to get things packed up.

I tried to get up and help, but Miri all joking aside pushed me back down to the ground. "Stay down, Gregor and I can get packed. You look like you did three days ago. Rest we've got a hard ride ahead of us."

I flumped back onto the ground, and then focused on Riley as he landed on my shoulder. "If you want to eat their eyes better do it now Riley. Cause we're leaving."

The Raven coughed distastefully and said, "Gnoll eyes? Please Sasha even I have standards."

Chapter 3

After our encounter with the Gnolls on the first night, we'd been left alone for the rest of the journey. Oh, we heard their horns in the forest and saw their scat on the road but that was it. We pushed our mounts and my body as far as they would allow us. The good news was because of the extra effort we arrived in the Principality of Ulm half a day behind the Company itself. We really couldn't have timed it better in fact. By the time we arrived, the thick earthworks had already been erected around the camp and the space for the tent Miri and I shared had been cleared and leveled.

That didn't mean we could sit back with our feet up of course, there was still plenty to do. First and foremost, taking care of our mounts, and then reporting to Roland. While many sellswords would have reversed the order; or allowed others to take care of their horses, Miri and I always cared for our horses personally. Neither of us wanted to put down another lame horse while being chased by bandits; because the stable boy the night before didn't care for the animal properly.

"Quite the camp," Gregor said as he rubbed down his mules as they munched quietly on the provided hey.

"Roland studied the classic texts of the Old Empire and organized his camps the same way. He's also a real bastard when it comes to discipline and rules," replied Miri. I was surprised at just how quickly the two of them bonded over the trip. They had spent most of the time through the Wald talking about their first fight and the Gnoll attack; going over every stroke with a level of detail that made both Riley and I fall asleep with boredom at different some points.

"I have to admit this is far more people than I was expecting," continued Gregor.

"The Company's a thousand-strong mixed force.

When you add specialists and camp followers there's around 1500 mortal inside the earthworks," I said as I finished rubbing down my horse. I was still a bit on the weak side, so I sat down on a bale of hey, to rest before I would start to brush it down.

"That's the problem with you city folk. Why not bring 1500 warriors instead of only a thousand?" Gregor asked dismissively. For the Pagan everyone who didn't use leaves to wipe their ass was a soft living 'city folk'.

"Because those thousand soldiers when properly supported can kick any three thousand Pagans in their collective asses," started Miri with conviction. "Our sharp end is seven hundred infantry, two hundred or so mounted troops and a battery of 4 light alchemical field guns. Most of the infantry are musketeers, but we have a hundred 'monster killers' as well. Roland was even able to convince a hundred Anglo mercenaries armed with their yew war bows to sign up."

"And we're really well equipped as well. Roland was able to purchase a thousand of the new flintlock muskets with the socket bayonets. The bayonets will allow a musketeer to deal with close in threats while still being able to keep up a steady rate of fire," I added not wanting to be left out of the conversation.

My comment caused Miri to snort in disbelief. "There's a large gulf between practice and theory Sasha, that's why Roland has the monster killers to fill that gulf."

Of course, Miri would mention those crazy bastards who filled the role she started her sellsword career in. Monster killers were fully armoured soldiers who were armed with greatswords, double handed bearded axes, and more varieties of polearms than anyone needed. Their role was to protect the musketeers from larger 'opponents' (Ogres, Trolls, really large Titan Spawn, Dragons etc.) that made it through the hail of 20mm musket balls, that the musketeer were unleashing every fifteen to twenty seconds.

126

"What of your cavalry?" asked Gregor.

"Half are dragoons, mounted infantry that serve as Roland's reserve. He can use them to exploit a breach in the enemy's line or shore up a hole in ours. For the other half we have a score of Hobgoblin hussars for scouts and two full squadrons of heavy cuirassiers. Those are the guys that will make the holes in the enemy's lines," replied Miri completely in her element. I know that she loved me, but Miri's first love will always be the where and how of warfare.

"Ba, it is a good thing I'm here. You talk like the Spawn will fight like other city folk. They won't, you want to fight them that means entering the woods, raiding and ambush," Gregor said unconvinced.

"Oh, trust me, we know that, but you can't expect a girl to give away all of her secrets on the first day," Miri said with an unexpectedly flirtatious voice.

"I've never found that to be the case," retorted Gregor. "Your city men must be doing something wrong,"

"True they don't use clubs," replied Miri with a wicked smile.

"Yes! You see Gregor is here for another reason. Show these city boys how to get women," Gregor said with a broad smile.

"Just be careful who you use as an example Gregor, Sasha and I aren't the only women around the camp that can hand you your ass," warmed Miri.

"Excellent! Can you point them out? I love hunting game that can bite back," the bearshirt said.

Now it was Miri's turn to laugh openly. "You're hopeless Gregor."

The big man just shrugged then seeing I was still winded from taking care of my horse walked over and picked up my saddle and tack. Stacking it on top of his own he lifted the load without effort and asked "Where to?"

And that was Gregor. He talked a rough game, was

course, but at the same time he was observant and gave a damn about the people around him. It hadn't taken long for the three of us to become good friends.

As we walked Gregor returned the conversation back to the Company, "Where do you two fit in?"

"Roland has a score or so soldants, 'independent' adventurers under his direct command. A few are spellcasters like Sasha, but mostly they're people who work best alone or as part of a small group: duelists, bodyguards, bounty hunters, monster hunters that sort of thing. Roland uses us to handle more complex problems that regular units lax the flexibility for.

Once we got to our tent site, Miri and Gregor insisted that I sit down and rest while they pitched the tent. I started to complain, but Miri shook her head and pointed to where our tack was piled.

"You look as pale as a ghost Sasha, let us do this then we can report in and get some food into you," said Miri. It had been close to a week since she'd fed, so she was in what I called her 'normal' period. In another week or so her mood would start to darken as the effects of her not feeding started to affect her personality.

I normally don't consider myself a lazy person, accept maybe when I'm in a warm bed on a cold morning; but I decided to let my two traveling companions pamper me for one more day. Besides watching two aggressive take charge warrior types try and work together to do something was just too much fun.

"Gregor how many times do I have to tell you nail the stakes in first before you raise the tent poles in," said an angry Miri.

Unfortunately, Gregor's response was drowned out by two rather loud squeals of delight as Sariel and Keira appeared and proceeded to race each other to see who would get to hug me and Miri first.

Sariel won and I found myself wrapped up in one rib

cracking hug quickly follow up by another.

"Sasha! It's been so long," said the Fey as if it had been five months, not five days since we'd seen each other. Maybe I was wrong about her being afraid of me. Or maybe Sariel wasn't in the mood to be afraid, right then.

"I missed you to Sariel," I replied to the blonde haired Fey, before adding, "You to Keira."

"Okay let her go before you crack her ribs again," ordered a rather put out Riley who had been comfortably snoozing on my shoulder before the latest ruckus.

I was quickly released by my two chastened friends who then quickly turned to embrace Miri with almost the same level of enthusiasm.

"Good evening ladies, I take it you are friends of Sasha and Miri?" asked Gregor as he straightened his crumpled and travel stained tunic.

Both of my friends turned to look at the bearshirt, surprise clearly evident upon both of their faces.

"Sasha isn't this one of the mortal sacrificing, girl stealing Pagans we fought last week?" asked Sariel for once not complaining.

"I've never sacrificed a human," started Gregor.

"Sariel, Keira; meet Gregor our newest recruit," I said cutting the big man off before things started to get really out of hand.

"I wasn't aware that Roland gave you permission to recruit new personnel," said Keira a hint of stubbornness in her voice.

"He didn't Keira, Gregor sort of volunteered, we were going to go meet with Roland as soon as we finished settling in," I replied

"Oh. Good, I'm sure Roland will want to hear the story behind his volunteering," said Keira her nose now definitely out of joint. Like many book mages Keira did not react well to the unexpected: especially when they couldn't fix (or blow up) the problem immediately.

"She's not the only one," said Sariel.

Chapter 4

"So, let me get this straight. You killed his boss: which in turn meant that the bearshirt found you interesting. As well, he feels that he's grown soft because Miri kicked his ass. Therefore, that is his reasoning for his wanting to join the Company and fight the Titan Spawn?" said Roland. Though his monotone voice didn't express any real emotion I could tell he was surprised by my story.

Both Miri and I were standing in Roland's command tent that had been resized to be in proportion to his great bulk. Square in shape, with each of the square having a smaller 'sub tent' it was Roland and Keira's work and living space. The central square was currently filled with a large map table surrounded by ten normal sized canvas folding chairs. Currently the table's surface reflected the full principality of Ulm, with our encampment glowing red, our employer forces blue and the possible Titan Spawn locations either a dark green or black.

"Well he's more following me and I think he'd be a good addition to the Company, but other than that yes you've pretty much got it," I said with a lot more confidence than I really felt.

"To be fair he could be a really be an asset Roland. From his stories he knows the Spawn, he certainly knows the woods, and after sparring with him for three days I think he's on the level," added Miri.

Roland turned his clockwork eyes towards my companion for several seconds, his face an unreadable mask. Turning back to me he said. "Alright he's hired; standard soldant wage," he said finally.

"Thank you, Roland, you'll not be sorry," I said relieved. Thinking the interview over I turned to leave.

"Hold on you two, we're not done yet. It appears that Sasha's little fight with the Pagan druid had reached the prince's ears. He's asked to meet the other two young

131

women who were responsible for defending his people before our next planning meeting, which is going to be two hours after dawn tomorrow. Get yourself cleaned up; Sariel has designed an official dress uniform for the soldants, I will expect both of you to be wearing it at the meeting," he said.

I was rather surprised how the words Sariel and uniform combined suddenly had me wishing to be back confronting the Pagans once more. However, I had concern right then, "What about Sariel? She was there as well," I asked.

"Oh, the Prince has already met Sariel, and she was very clear that you two did all the work, and that her role was, how did she put it again, 'too small to be any consequence'," said Roland.

Chapter 5

So, the uniform that Miri and I had to wear was pretty much everything that I feared. Sariel had been talking to Roland and the other sellswords about the current fashions for military uniforms and had felt that given the heroic and free-wheeling nature of the soldants; apparently, I had been a bad influence in this area, our uniforms should be based upon an equally flamboyant and romantic group: which was why I was currently dressed like a Hobgoblin Hussars.

My Dwarven upbringing has been a blessing in many ways but one of its downsides has been the prejudice that I instinctively feel towards the Goblinoid races. Yes, the roots of that prejudice are pretty justified, but a lot of time has passed since those roots were anywhere close to relevant. Especially in the today's Imperium: now that the Hobgoblin Consul was also an Elector who in theory could actually become the Kaiser. Still wearing something on based upon a Hobgoblin uniform caused me to have a negative opinion of it right from the start.

The good news was that the typical Hobgoblin was slighter in build than a typical human male so the basic shape actually suited a female form more than other choices. Unfortunately, Sariel being Sariel, the uniforms were tight.

The breeches were black silk, reinforced in the crotch and inner thighs by black leather. Thick interwoven red and silver braiding ran down the outer side of the legs and all of this was shoved into tight, knee high shiny black riding boots. The dolman jacket was a reverse in colour from the breeches being red silk with enough black braiding and silver buttons to stop a sword cut. As if that wasn't enough, over our left arm and shoulder we wore a second, pelisse, jacket of thick red silk with even more black braiding. Both the breeches and the dolman were cut to make it very clear that Miri and I were women and if I actually had to move with any sort of speed I was positive something would have split. However, what made me really hate the uniform was that my trusted and beloved tricorne hat was replaced by a black and red shako that required a strap to actually keep it in place. I could forgive Sariel many things but having to give up my tricorne that had kept my head dry and warm for close to five years crossed a line.

"It's only for formal occasions Sasha, most of the time you won't be wearing the damned hat anyways," Riley had finally pointed out to me in an attempt to stop my bitching. "Just wear the damned thing and lump it."

On the bright side, they were military uniforms, so unlike our dresses from the party, weapons were completely acceptable as accessories. I was wear both Thunder and Lightning, though both had to be on my left side, and Miri wore her Old Empire sword and dagger. The longsword had to stay on her horse for the visit.

Which is how two hours later; Miri and I found ourselves, along with Roland, Keira, and several of his staff officers riding up to the Prince's Keep. Five Cuirassiers, acting as an honor guard, rounded out the procession. I was surprised to see that Keira was dressed in the same hussar inspired uniform. That she was wearing something other than her, normally stained, green dress was surprising enough. What was truly shocking however, was that the book mage had bathed, and her now clean hair was done up in a loose Elf braid. It was the most presentable that I'd ever seen Keira and showed that if she had tried the book mage could turn heads if she wanted to. When I quietly asked Roland about the transformation he just rumbled something about Sariel playing 'fairy god sister again' and turned his attention back to our destination.

I was feeling almost normal after a night sleeping where I wasn't keeping one ear open; so I was able listen to Keira's small talk. Mind you, Keira being Keira, her small talk was really a lecture about the land we were going to protect. "The Principality is just over 1,500 square kilometres in size including the parts now covered by the Titan Wald, but the area that's cultivated is less than 1,000 kilometres," she started.

I let out a low whistle; I could walk across the land in one day. There wasn't a lot of space to give ground if we had to. But that so typical of the Imperium; it was a dog's breakfast of kingdoms, free cities, dukedoms, principalities, counties, Dwarf mountains, Elven glades, and Dragon holds. All held together by a Kaiser who was supposed to be elected by and from a group of 20 mortals who along with arm's length of other titles also bore the title Electors. No one sane would have ever created the Imperium like this if they'd been starting from scratch. But the Imperium had never been 'created'; it just sort of 'grew' this way.

"Yes, you're correct it is quite small, but then that's why the Company can conceivably defend it," said Keira answering my unasked question. How she could pick up on that social cue and not others were beyond me.

"The Titan Wald has encroached Ulm on three sides including the mountains to the Northwest. This is where we expect the Titan Spawn to attack. Only the lands to the east that border the River resemble the landscape the way that it looked before the great dying."

My friend was speaking at an even greater speed then normal: excited that someone was actually paying attention to her.

Looking around, I saw that the farmland we rode through was uneven, pitted with the holes of uprooted trees that hadn't been adequately filled in, or the tree stumps still present. It was clear that the people of Ulm had fought the Titan Wald to a standstill and were still fighting. I liked that stiff necked stubbornness in people. Right then I knew that I was going to like these citizens of Ulm and I was glad I was going to help defend them.

However, it wasn't just trees that had scarred the

landscape. As we rode; we passed through two abandoned and partially demolished villages. Such sites were common enough now a days but what bothered me was just how recent the villages looked abandoned. My best guess was that these had been inhabited as late as this spring. I saw several small orchards of a dozen or so trees that still were heavy with unpicked fruit, along with vegetable gardens unharvested and going to seed.

"Where are all the people?" I asked Keira interrupting her train of words.

My friend paused before responding. To her credit Keira didn't mind being interrupted mid lecture, especially with questions relevant to the topic at hand.

"The Prince of Ulm has suspected that the Titan Spawn were going to attack in force since this spring. He felt that this time it wasn't just going to be a few raids but a major invasion. So he evacuated the villages and had the people move to the region around the keep. They've been building fortifications all summer and much of the fall," explained Keira.

Then in a quieter voice she added, "He's been extending the robota as much as possible, forcing the people to farm his fields and build the fieldworks. The villagers protested and have sent letters to the Kaiser but so far nothing has come from it."

I nodded in understanding but not agreement. Robota was the obligated labour many Imperium citizens still owed their lords. Before the Red Death it had largely died out as a practice being replaced by higher taxes. Since the plague though, labour has become more valuable than gold for many landlords so the practice had returned.

As Keira lectured on about Ulm's major exports, I continued to look about; incorporating what Keira had told me with what I saw around me. The large fields around the keep and abandoned villages had not only been harvested but had been prepared properly for the heavy winter snows.

Obviously, the fields belonged to the Prince while the neglected orchards and vegetable gardens had been the villagers.

As the keep came into view, I saw that all of the villager's efforts hadn't been completely wasted. As we got closer it became clear that the keep's walls had been neglected and actually deconstructed over the past decades. However, this summer had been used to an attempt to reverse the damage that had been done. Newly shaped stone, several shades darker than the keep's original stone works, had been used to repair the main wall and the turrets. The gates were built using fresh green wood, and even a kilometre out I could sense the magic presence of defensive rituals protecting those inside the keep from hostile magic.

But it wasn't just the keep that had been worked on. Fifty metres out from the old wall, was another wall. The new fortification was a thick wood and rubble wall that was perhaps seven metres in height and three metres across, with a wooden fighting platform every twenty metres or so. While it may not have been sturdy as the keep; the new wall looked solid enough to at least slow down a Spawn attack. Although I had to hope that it could do more than that because between the outer and inner walls were several dozen hastily constructed buildings that I guess were meant to house the villagers left homeless by the Princes orders.

It all looked impressive to my eye but I wasn't the military expert of the team. Leaning over to Miri I asked, "What do you think of the Prince's efforts?"

"The Prince had better hope we kill all the Minotaurs in the Spawn's army because they'll just step over that wooden wall and punch through the stone one. The Company could take the keep in half a day with just our alchemical cannon and they were meant for field work not siege craft," she replied

"The Prince had few options and this was better than

nothing," said Roland overhearing our conversation.

Both points of view were nothing new to me. Since the great dying, nobles of all stripes had been trying to hold onto what they considered theirs. Invariably it was the peasants and city freemen who paid the price for the noble's folly. On the other hand, people had a right to defend themselves and their homes, it just seemed strange to me to have to destroy your home first and then try and defend it.

"Have you met the Prince?" I asked Keira, deciding I'd hold off making any judgements until after I'd met the man.

"I haven't, but Roland has met with him on a daily basis. He thinks well of the Prince, so I'm inclined to give him the benefit of the doubt," she replied.

I nodded in understanding. Roland was no fool so I decided to follow Keira's lead on this matter until I met him myself.

As we passed through the outer gates we got off our horses and walked them along a corduroy road that lead indirectly to the keep's gatehouse. Taking the time to look around I saw hundreds of mortals all busy at work: buildings were being constructed, the wooden wall was completed, and the sound of multiple anvils being hit by hammers was heard throughout. On the wind, along with all the 'pleasant' smells associated with a town, I could sense the use of magic. It was reasonably strong and consisted of multiple casting layered one on top of each other. Taken as a hole it offered a reasonably effective magical defence, but one that would take time to rebuild if damaged.

The road twisted between buildings preventing a straight passage between the outer wall and the keep. As we made one turned we came upon one of the few open areas between the walls. There militia drilled with polearms, while, under a broad tent, children dutifully worked on creating musket cartridges.

On the one hand I was impressed, by what I saw. Everyone seemed calm, and there was no sense of panic, but I still felt that something was wrong.

"They're all quiet. There's no gossiping, no jokes, no banter, even the children are quiet," said Miri.

I had to agree with Miri there was still the sound of voices, people giving orders or instructions, but those singular voices made the silence of everyone else even more pronounced.

"They think that they've no hope of living. Their plan now is selling their lives as dearly as possible," said Riley a note of anger in his voice.

"Keira just what sort of one-way mission have we signed up for? Cause if the locals think they're dead then what hope does the Company have?" I asked the book mage.

"A good one Sasha; because we're the ones bringing the hope. Hard choices have been made, and the foundation for a victory has been laid. It's up to us to show all these mortals that they have a good chance, a fighting chance, to survive and see next spring," interrupted Roland.

Before I could say anything a couple of children who had broken away from the tent came running up to Roland.

"Excuse me Hauptmann sir, is she here?" the oldest, a human girl just on the verge of womanhood, asked.

"Yes, she is, can you tell which one?" Roland asked, holding up one hand to halt the column.

The two of them were soon joined by three others, and all of them started whispering back and forth.

Finally one of them, a red haired dwarf boy whose beard had barely started to grow in, pointed at Miri. "I bet it was that one, my vator says all Elves have magic."

"It's not her! The stories say that she had silver hair, that one has red hair," said another boy with an all knowing tone that only a child can truly pull off without sounding like a pompous ass.

"Besides she's carrying a sword, everyone knows magic users don't use swords," said an expert in magical lore.

"You're mostly right, though I'd be talking in a more respectful about anyone who's armed with a sword. It's a good life lesson," started Roland he then pointed at me and continued. "She's the wild mage that defeated the druid in Letzte Moglichkeit.

I suddenly was the centre of attention for a dozen young eyes. A few were filled with sudden fear, but most were wide eyed, one of them shouted "it's her: the wild mage is here."

And then it was all chaos, as a score of children suddenly appeared and these were soon followed by at least as many adults. They were all staring at me with such desperate looks upon their faces that I started to take a step back confused.

"Don't back away," whispered Riley "Take off your hat and bow to the people."

I did as Riley suggested and was met with a surprising round of cheers and applause, from the still growing crowd.

"Well I'm sure my friend would love and stay to tell you all about her fight, but I'm afraid that we have an appointment with the Prince and we have to press on," said Roland amplifying his voice without actually shouting. He then motioned for the rest of us to start moving again.

As we did so I moved up to walk beside my commander.

"What was that all about?" I asked.

"As I said yesterday, the news of your fight with the Pagans reached Ulm before we did. It's been a while since someone stood up to any Titan worshipers so when they heard that a mage actually defeated a Pagan druid; everyone wanted to hear more. When I found out, I made sure that everyone knew it was one of the sellswords that were coming to help them," explained Roland.

"I'm confused I thought you said that my defeating the druid by myself was bad for morale?" I asked.

"I still think that, but I played the hand as I was dealt it. The important thing was that a Titan believer was defeated. Would I have preferred the story of that defeat involved a group of mortals working together yes: but if all I have to work with is the story of a powerful hero using raw power to win, then I'll make as much of that as possible to give people hope. Now enough we're about to meet the Prince and his advisors," replied Roland as he started to once again move towards the keep.

Chapter 6

Unlike the outer fortifications, the keep seemed rather still as we entered. Oh, there were a hundred or so people in the courtyard that should have been doing something. Instead they were still and looking at Roland's party. Well to be honest they were all looking at me.

"I think they knew you were coming," whispered Miri to me. My lover was having entirely too much fun at my expense.

"Fuck you," I whispered back.

"Promise?" Miri responded.

"Children, not now," chided Riley taking the role of the adult this time.

We shut up as a stuffy nobleman entered the courtyard from one of the side buildings.

My reply was cut off as a stuffy nobleman entered the courtyard from one of the side buildings.

"Ah Hauptmann Roland, nice to see that you are on time," he said looking down his nose at Roland while at the same time looking up at the Golem's head 50 centimetres above his own. The nobleman then tilted his head and look directly at Miri and I with the same level of distain that he'd shown Roland. "I take it that these are the young women that the Prince wishes to meet?"

I very carefully kept my face as neutral as possible. I hated these kinds of mortals, the kinds that think just because they were born a noble that they were better than everyone else. All races have them, even people are well grounded as the Dwarves, but I still try to avoid them as best as I can.

"Yes," said Roland as he gestured me forward and said. "Manfred von Gott may I present Frauleins Sasha Storm Crow and Miri."

The noble man snapped his heels together and gave us a short bow. "Frauleins please follow me, Hauptmann you

142

and the rest of your personnel can wait in the officer's mess until the Prince is ready for you.

Von Gott turned and started to walk towards what I guessed were the Prince's quarters, without even thinking that the two of us wouldn't follow.

I waited until he took three steps before I started after him, making sure that my jackets were straight and that I'd looked my best. Even Riley took a couple of steps down my shoulder so that he could straighten up and look properly 'Raven like'.

As we entered the receiving room von Gott waited for the two of us, so that he could provide a thirty second course on etiquette. "Keep your hands in front or behind your back; never by your side or close to your weapons. No talking or even moving of your lips unless asked a direct question. Curtsy when either entering or leaving the prince's presence; or when you see me bow. You do know how to curtsy do you not?"

"Yes, my aunt," I started.

"A simple yes or no will suffice for most questions. In the unlikely event that a question requires more than either of those two words keep your answers as short as possible. Never turn your back to the Prince. Finally, and most importantly absolutely do not cast any magic while in the prince's or his family's presence. Do you understand?" he continued as if these instructions were the passwords to the Imperium's treasure vault.

"Yes," I answered deciding that playing the game was the fastest way to get out of this mad house with my head intact.

Miri just nodded her head in the affirmative.

"Excellent," he said as we finally stopped before a human size set of double doors that smelled of recently cast magic. "The prince is within; wait here until the doors are opened and you are announced," said the chamberlain before opening the doors and entering himself.

As the doors were opened I heard the sound of a woman engaged in a heated argument with someone. I didn't find out who because the doors closed and the magic spell, I guessed of silence, reinstated itself and I couldn't hear anything else from the room.

"Give me the word and I'll shit all over that powered wig of his," said Riley.

I suppressed a grin, and gave the Raven an affectionate rub under his chin. Where would I be without him? Even more than Miri, Riley had been through thick and thin with me, and even now he helped me face an uncomfortable situation with courage and a clear head.

After several seconds the door opened again and I heard von Gott say, "May I present to your majesties: the saviors of the village of Letzte Moglichkeit. Sasha Storm Crow, a wild mage in the employ of Hauptmann Roland and Miri an Elven warrior also in the employ of the Hauptmann.

Taking a deep breath and with a quick glace to Miri for support, I entered the room.

Chapter 7

My first reaction when I finally enter the presence of the man who was royalty, the ruler of this land and ultimately my employer was…underwhelming. The prince was a short balding human whose wrinkly, red marked face showed the result to much tobacco and even more drink. He stood as I came in, but he was still stooped, his shoulders hunched forward as if he'd be bearing a great weight for far too long. His clothes had clearly been slept in and judging by the aroma in the room hadn't been changed in some time. It was only when our eyes met that I felt like I was in the presence of someone who actually ruled. Those dark eyes held me frozen in place as effective as any vampire I'd ever met. I was assessed, my traits weighed and it appeared that I was found wanting; and by how the magic felt in this room I realized that no one that this man had met ever measured up to his standards.

His private chamber was much like him. Every open book shelf and table space groaned under the weight of leather bound books, scrolls, and endless pieces of paper. However, there was an order to it all that was not to be underestimated.

Next to the prince, stood a much younger woman who, either because of lifestyle or magic, was much healthier in appearance. Tall, straight backed and dressed the latest fashion, she was out of place within the room. It was only in the eyes that I saw that she and the prince were related. Right now her face was flush and it was clear that she was the one who the prince had been arguing with.

Initial assessments and disappointments past, the prince clipped his heels together and gave Miri and me a slight nod of the head.

"Fraulien Storm Crow, Fraulien Miri may I present His Royal Highness, Prince Kilian Friz Erhart Ulm: The Prince of Ulm, Arch Duke of Kalmar, Duke of Asdorf,

Duke of Selina,"

At the third duke ship the Prince gave von Gott a look indicating that was enough of his pedigree.

Von Gott cleared his throat and then continued "And his recognized heir, her Grace the Lady Adela Eva Lucia Ulm."

I did my best to curtsy to both, wishing I had had time to practice more.

"So you're the young women who broke the power of the Pagans within the southern part of my realm?" asked the Prince, his language was stilted a bit, as if he wasn't quite sure how to address a commoner who was also a mage.

"Yes Sir," I said. Keeping my answer's short as I'd been instructed seemed like a good idea.

Miri as was our usual procedure, kept silent and let me do all the talking.

"The Pagans have been growing bolder since our attention has been drawn north. Your actions appear to have checked them somewhat. And since we've found out that all of you were women, my daughter has wanted to meet you. Apparently, you're her new heroines for the common people, who is meant to protect them from all the monsters both inside and outside the principality," Said Prince Kilian.

"Father!" said Princess Adela shocked.

"So, what say you mage? Am I, a monster for demanding my due from my people? For having them focus on what needs to be focused on to survive the winter? For hiring mercenaries and keeping them fed while those that have lived here for generations may starve?" asked the old man.

I should have stayed silent. Roland would have wanted me to stay silent. However, when I came into my magic, my Dwarf aunts made sure that I knew how to speak truth to power, and my Dwarf uncles made sure I knew how to

146

stand up to bullies. Fortunately, before I could say anything Princess Adela intervened.

"Don't answer that Frauline Storm Crow. Shame on you father, here are two people who did you a service and you try and bait them with a crime of treason just because I think their actions are praise worthy," she said directing her barbs towards her father.

Damn them both. We were tools for them both; to use against each other. Well either Miri or I were tools; time for me to get us out of this quagmire.

"He could try Milady, but I believe he's taken our measure and that of Hauptmann Roland. His Highness knows that if he tried to have us arrested, that we would only go if we chose to. As well he knows the good Hauptmann would just march in, breaking ever wall, door, and person that stood between us and freedom," I said as I locked eyes with the Prince himself. I realized that this was a man long used to facing the reality of a situation. "And we would meet him half way. After, we'd take apart this little realm getting our due wage and leave the rest for the Spawn."

The room was silent. No one could believe that I just threatened the entire principality. I felt von Gott stiffen beside me waiting for the expected explosion, and Miri tensed beside me. However, Prince Kilian broke into a smile and then he started to laugh. Given the reaction of von Gott and Princess Adela this was something that was uncharacteristic for the Prince.

"Finally, we have some honesty in the room! Thank you Frauline; it's been weeks since someone had the balls to tell me the obvious facts of a situation. You are correct I do have your Hauptmann Roland's measure and what you describe is very much what would happen, or at least both of you and he would try. But he is not the first mercenary Hauptmann I've dealt with, nor are you the first mage," said the Prince and he sat down in his stiff-backed chair.

147

"Von Gott: wine and fresh glasses, and breakfast rations for two," he said to the Chamberlain. Turning back to me he continued. "I'm afraid due to the current crisis I have little to offer right now but my official thank you. My land is besieged and hard decisions have had to been made for everyone survival. However, if there is a reasonable boon that I could offer in the future please do not hesitate to ask."

Feeling that the interview was winding down, I started to relax.

I stiffened back up again when there was a firm but unexpected knock on the door that for some reason caused a shiver to run down my spine, and Riley to flutter nervously.

The door opened and in walked a dead man.

"Ah see that I am not too late, excellent," said the walking corpse. His speech was crisp and clear. Whatever magic was being used to keep him moving preserved much of his vocal cords as well.

A brief look of distaste passed over Prince Kilian's face but it was soon replaced with the emotional mask that had been on when I had entered the room. "Citizen Stain, I do not remember requesting an audience," he said formally.

"I invited him father. He expressed an interest in meeting Frauline Storm Crow and her companion as well. I saw no harm with the request," said Princess Adela.

Stain turned and his face Miri and I and with a tone of a sated hunger said, "Frauline Storm Crow, and Citizen Miri. I had hoped that the descriptions from the stories were true."

It moved toward me extending his hand.

Suddenly Miri was in front of me: eyes red and fangs out. "Back off dead man," she said speaking for the first time. She hadn't drawn a weapon but her body language made it clear that she was ready for a fight.

"Frauline Miri! Citizen Stain is the accredited

ambassador from the Phoenix Republic, as long as you are in the employ of Ulm you shall give him the respect that his station demands," said the Princess angrily.

"Oh, that is alright, your Highness, the Citizen has long been known for her seditious thoughts and her disloyalty to the ideas that the Republic stand for. It is not surprising that her greetings would be less than polite," Citizen Stain said to the heir of Ulm.

Turning his attention back Miri, he said, "In the case that warrior in question was you, I've been instructed to convey both of your parents' love and to let you know they are both well. They hope you will soon tire of this foolish rebelliousness and look forward to seeing you reunited with your true family.

That was the politest threat I've ever had leveled against me, but it still caused several fractures in my emotional calm. I didn't move and I think I kept my face emotionless, but there were several gentle gusts of wind that kicked up papers and dust within the Prince's room. Static electricity started to arch between me and Riley.

The sudden smell of ozone in the room caused everyone to pause their actions. Miri might have been a Daywalker and an immense physical threat, but I had just reminded everyone why I had been summoned to meet the Prince, and thoughts of being torn apart by tornado strength winds suddenly gained a whole new realism.

For the first time Citizen Stain realized that Miri wasn't the only threat he faced in the room and took a step back. Princess Adela had lost almost all of her colour as she, perhaps for the first time, realized just how over her head she was in a physical power sense.

The Prince on the other hand registered approval. It was clear that he didn't like Citizen Stain that much either and took my and Miri's reaction to him as a loss of standing. "I believe that we've kept you both here long enough, Frauline Storm Crow, you have my permission to leave."

Turning to the Prince, I curtsied once more and backed out of the room before I lost my last pieces of self-control, Miri did much the same with a genuine, fangs in, smile to the Prince. As the door closed and I felt it was safe to breathe again, I began to see why Roland liked the man.

Chapter 8

Over the next two of weeks we established ourselves within the Principality and started building a plan for the defence against the Spawn.

As part of our patrols I suggested to Roland that we harvest as much from the gardens and orchards as we could. I argued that if we did so, and returned most of it to the local population that we'd garner a lot of good will with the villagers. Roland thought that was an excellent idea and took it several steps further. We'd been given hunting rights over the Principality to supplement our supply situation. As a result, the Company had harvested quite a bit of the local animal life. Of course, Keira being Keira, she knew a food preservation ritual that worked, not only on, fruits and vegetables but meat as well. So along with the preserved carrots, turnips, several types of squash, peas, and a few other vegetables that were far to healthy for me to eat regularly, we distributed several hundred kilograms of dried deer, rabbit, and wild fowl back to the very people who had started to grow it in the first place.

"You do know that I blow things up better than you right?" I joked at one point with Keira as she finished casting yet another refined version of her preservation ritual upon half a tonne of fruits and vegetables.

"You've never seen my fireball, have you?" replied the book mage with a smile of such supreme confidence, it had caused me to suddenly feel very inadequate as a mage.

"This is what many male mortals would describe as a ball shrinking moment," said Riley rather smugly.

"What is your obsession with small round objects?" I asked as I went to find something to do to make me feel useful.

A day later I was helping the cavalry troopers to train their replacement mounts not to react to loud noises. They would ride their mounts in formation around the training field and I'd release a clap of thunder or bolt of lightning every now and then. They'd then had to take the next few minutes getting their mounts under control. It was good training for everyone. The horses got used to sudden loud noises, the rider's got practice controlling skittish mounts, and I was working myself back up to being able to channel magic for extended periods of time. We were on a short break, and I was enjoying my payment for helping: all the coffee I could drink and as many pretzels as I could scoff down, when Riley landed on my shoulder.

"Sasha, are you eating pretzels?" he asked with a certain joy in his voice.

My familiar loves the doughy crossed rings almost as much as he loves eyes. Especially when I roll pieces of them into balls; really, he's obsessed with the shape. I broke a piece off rolled it between my hands and threw it in his general direction. Without moving his feet off of my shoulder he'd grabbed it out of the air and swallowed it whole.

"I believe we're about to be visited by Royalty again," said Riley as he finished his baked goodness.

Turning; I saw that the Princess Adela and several of her ladies in waiting and an equally large number of guards had ridden up to our practise field. Having caught my eye, I saw one of her ladies waving me over. Putting down my coffee, and picking up my great coat, I walked over to where she was making sure I was presentable by the time I was close enough to have a conversation without shouting.

"Your Highness. How may I serve you today?" I asked as I curtsied.

"Walk with me," she replied as she dismounted. Her companions moved to dismount as well, only to be waved back into their saddles by the Princess. Only the guard captain and two of his men continued to dismount; pulling out flintlock carbines from their saddles as they did so.

Giving the three men an exasperated look, but

remaining silent as she walked up to me, the Princess gestured to the side of the training ground that was much less muddy.

After a minute of walking in silence the Princess said "I wanted to offer my thanks and the thanks of my people for saving the harvest of their own lands. It was a gesture of true goodwill, that was unexpected by many."

"It was the Captain who gave the orders you should be thanking him," I said.

"I did, and he suggested that I thank you as well. He said that it was your idea," she replied with a brilliant smile.

I had to admit being smiled at by a Princess was quite the rush.

"I have tried on several occasions to convince my father to reduce the robota and allow the people to return to their own lands to gather what food that they could, but he refused. He's convinced that the Titan Spawn will attack after the first snow and wants his land to be as well defended as possible. Even if that means that the people who call this land home starve as a result," she said.

"I take it you feel otherwise," I said carefully. Even I recognized that this conversation was getting dangerous.

"I believe that we must be open to new things. We are in a new world today and that it requires new thinking. My father is very traditional in his thinking and believes that if it worked before it will work again. But; if something has never been tried before; its suspect, and not to be trusted. Before the Great Dying and the Madness, his ideas may have been sound: but now? I fear he is out of his depth," she continued.

"I see," I said with caution. From what I had observed, the Prince had a good grasp of things, and based upon our first meeting it was the Princess herself that was in over her head.

The Princess smiled again, "Don't worry Lady Storm

Crow I do not expect you to do anything. I really did just come here to thank you and your Hauptmann for showing that often there is a third choice if you're willing to look for it.

"You are most welcome M'lady," I said; then my heart added before my brain could stop it, "and if there is anything else I could do for you, you have but to ask."

The Princess gave me a very knowing smile but remained silent as we walked back to her entourage. As her Captain walked past me he gave me such a strong look of 'back off' that I almost took a step backwards.

"Oh, you do love walking into bear's dens don't you," asked Riley once they left. "First you listen to her criticism of her father, and then you openly flirt with her."

"Flirt? I didn't flirt with her," I defended myself while only slightly blushing,

"'And if there's anything else I can do for you please let me know.' She said as she batted her big blue eyes. Oh yeah you weren't flirting at all," he said pointedly.

Okay so maybe I was flirting a bit, but I mean seriously Princess; who wouldn't be flirting with one?

Chapter 9

As winter was really starting to hit Roland had his soldants and dragoons start to patrol more aggressively along the border between the forest and the settled lands. Which is how Gregor, Miri and I ended up on a two-day foot patrol along the border about five hundred metres into the forest. Sariel did not join us on this patrol. Since she and the rest of the Company had arrived in Ulm, Roland had found the Fey to be too valuable in a liaison role. A novelty to noble and peasant alike, whomever Roland sent her to see, Sariel always got the results that our commander wanted.

We'd packed light for the patrol since we were travelling through pretty thick forest without mounts. We took only a few days' worth of food and water along with extra warm clothing, bedding and as many pairs of stockings that our magical bags of holding could hold. Since this wasn't a situation where a dress uniform was needed I was grateful to be back in my standard greatcoat and tricorne hat. We did however change our footwear from heeled riding boots to hobnailed campaigning boots. While I missed the extra two inches in height; not slipping every tenth step in difficult terrain was a definite advantage.

Along with our old clothing we were of course armed to the teeth. Along with her longsword, Miri had packed her Old Empire short sword, at least two daggers, half a dozen throwing spikes and one of Sariel's pistols. Along with his ax, and several daggers that could have been easily been called short swords, Gregor also embraced enough 'city ways' to now carry a flintlock blunderbuss. That my two companions carried gunpowder weapons around me showed just how strong the potential of danger was on this patrol. I only bothered with Thunder and Lightning, as like any other mage would boast 'I am my own best weapon'.

Animals that were interested in the crops in the

cultivated lands and mortals who were interested in the wood, herbs, and wild game found within the forest had worn tracks that went into and out of the Wald on a fairly regular basis. Unfortunately, our patrols took us across those natural pathways. So we had to walk through a lot of virgin forest, as quietly as possible. I emphasise the word quietly here because I made more noise than my other two companions together. Gregor combined his Pagan magic with years of experience moving through forest to pass through the thickets and shrubs like they weren't there. Miri used a combination of her parent's heritages to either noiselessly squirm, or leap over whatever obstacle that blocked her path. Me, being a mere 'city born' human ended up battling my way through the forest; with the forest often, good giving as it got. On more than one occasion I just said screw it and flew up and over whatever obstacle that blocked my path. I often had to endure the strained looks from my two companions; as I landed with the after effects of the spell echoing around me.

Fortunately, our luck held for almost the entire trip and while we encountered plenty of signs of the Titan Spawn passing along the tracks we'd not encountered any actual Spawn. Our luck though finally broke just as our patrol was winding down.

The first star was just becoming visible in the eastern sky as we approached the remains of one of the outlying villages that the Prince had evacuated earlier in the year. Roland had stationed a squad of ten Dragoons there as part of an early warning defence of the Principality. The fortified position was the ultimate goal for the three (four if you include Riley) of us and we were all looking forward to a hot meal and more importantly hot coffee. The first snow that was actually staying on the ground was falling and the only way I was keeping warm was by staying on the move.

Because our goal now was the village, we could actually use one of the deer tracks to move, which meant that we were actually making reasonable time. We stayed alert to danger however, given our luck the last thing we expected was things to go as planned. So, when Gregor held up one arm as a signal to freeze neither Miri nor I were that surprised. He then sniffed the air and pointed down to the border of the forest. I turned to Miri only to see that she gave me a look of revulsion that I only understood after several seconds; when the smell of rotten, well everything also hit me. Titan Spawn were in the area.

As quietly as possible we moved to the edges of the track, ready to bolt in if more Spawn were moving down the track towards us. Finally, after what seemed like hours, with no one coming we started to slowly move down the track to the forest's edge. After several minutes of further movement, we saw the outline of our first Titan Spawn emerge out of the gloom. This was followed by another and a third.

These Spawn were known as Hornmen, and they were a very different group then the Gnolls that we'd tangled in our ride up here. Instead of a mixture of wolf, dog and mortals, these Spawn appeared to be a mixture of goat, sheep, cattle and mortals: with long herbivore faces, cloven hooves and a wide variety of horns, which is the reason for their rather uncreative name. They were armed and armoured in a similar fashion to the Gnolls however: with crude, cleaver like swords and axes, stone spears and metal banded clubs, for weapons and ill cured hides mixed with leather for armour and thick wooden shields for defence. All of their possessions were covered with dried blood, shit, rust and several other substances that I really didn't want to know more about.

We all froze, while Miri and Gregor, whose eyes were far better in the forest's murk than mine, looked around. It was just blind luck we'd run into the warband and not the other way around. Now they were between us and our goal; less than six hundred metres away from the Dragoon's

157

position who despite the smell didn't even know they were there.

To make matters worse, we could hear a constant stream of quiet guttural sounds in front of us. Not for the first time I wished I had Keira's flexibility with magic. I'm sure the book mage had a comprehend languages spell within her mix of magic or at the very least a way of communicating without others hearing you. But I didn't have that kind of fast casting spell magic; I could only control the elemental forces of nature.

What I did have however, were friends who could think on their feet, and right then I'd take that over fancy magic. Gregor got all of our attentions and then pointed towards the Dragoon camp. He then made an X in the grass. Then he pointed to all the Spawn in front of us, who thankfully hadn't seen us yet, and made a bunch of shallow holes in the dirt. Finally, he pointed at the three of us, including Riley as he pointed towards me, and made another X. With a series of quick gestures, he then indicated that he believed that the Hornmen were going to attack the camp soon. However, we should wait until they did attack and then hit them from behind. Or at least I thought that's what his gestures and map indicated. I'd have to check once we'd started to move.

So, we sat there for what seemed like hours, while the sun's final glow faded and night truly fell. It became so black that I couldn't see a thing in the woods. Then we started to hear movement as the Spawn started to crawl slowly out of the forest and onto the winter fields. Still we stayed motionless. After several more long minutes all we heard was the deep rustle of the branches in the night breeze.

"Alright, I think Spawn have gone," whispered Gregor finally. He waited several seconds to see if his words caused alarms. Sensing no change, he continued with growing glee, "You three ready to screw them up?"

158

I nodded and then realizing I couldn't see Miri or Riley I whispered, "Yes."

"That's better. Move to side of the forest and wait until I cause commotion then start to run like a really big demon was chasing you. Try and get to city horse soldier's camp. Get them out of here. Spawn raiding for show and try to scare metal Captain. We're going to scare them instead," Gregor said. He sounded like he was looking forward to the fight.

"How many Hornmen are we dealing with?" I asked.

"I saw about thirty around us so maybe another twenty past those," said Miri.

"Fifty to Hundred in normal warband: sounds right for raid like this," agreed Gregor.

"So best case, we're outnumbered 5 to 1," I said. "Riley it should be safe to fly up to a branch and take a look at the Spawn's progress."

Without a word I felt the raven take off from my shoulder. I loosened Thunder and Lightning from their sheaths waiting from my familiar's return. I didn't have to wait long, as he landed first on my Tricorne and then hopped onto my shoulder. "They're about a third of the way there and the dragoons haven't seen them. They've posted a couple of guards but it seems that they are more interested in evening chores and making sure they've a warm place to sleep than being attacked," he reported once he settled himself in place.

"Right time to screwup the Spawn's plans. Wait here and don't hit me with any daggers or spells," Gregor warned us both.

I then felt the bearshirt move off into the night leaving me alone with both Miri and Riley.

"Okay both of you are faster than me in situations like this. When the time comes get to the camp and get them moving out," Miri said to Riley and I. She hadn't fed for several weeks so her Daywalker speed was reduced to only

159

slightly faster than a mortal Elf.

"If you think I'm just going to leave you," I started a little too loud; I then felt Miri's small but rough hand over my mouth.

"Of course, you're not going to leave me. I'd have carved my way to you by then and that way we can all take off when I get there she replied.

"Oh," I said now feeling foolish. Feeling like saying anything more would just get me into more trouble I started to move to the forest's edge and waited for Gregor to start.

Chapter 10

I admit I was expecting Gregor's 'signal' to be his blunderbuss going off, so even I was startled by what sounded like the roar of a large brown bear, perhaps twenty-five metres from me. The goat and sheep headed Spawn were startled as well. Whether mutant or not, I challenge any mortal not to react to the roar of a bear within its charge range. Their reaction was sudden and hardly surprising. Many of the Hornmen jumped up ready to defend themselves from the bear attack.

Only when Gregor had a large number of clear targets did he fire off the blunderbuss sending ten pistol balls flying hopefully into a pack of the monsters. I didn't know for sure, because I had to focus on my own job now.

With her own much higher pitched shriek Miri charged into the nearest pack of Hornmen. She'd drawn her longsword and its magic blade glowed dimly through the gloom of the new night. Just before she charged home, I channeled magical energy through Thunder, and caused a clamp of thunder to hit the group of creatures that she was aiming at. Thanks to months of working together I'd timed the spell perfectly. Miri smashed into the Hornmen while they were still completely stunned by the spell's aftereffects. Miri made the most of my distraction and cut down two of the Hornmen before they were aware that she was even there. Then she was gone, deeper into the Goatmen's line and out of my limited mortal sight.

Now it was my turn to get going. My first problem? How was I going to get through an alerted line of Titan Spawn and not get bogged down? Fortunately, this was exactly what my thunder leap spell was designed to solve.

I started to channel and store the necessary magical energy for the spell in both Thunder and Lightning as I ran towards the still stunned group of Hornmen that Miri had just plowed her way through. Then when I was close enough to touch them, I released the magic into the spell.

The clap of thunder I released was powerful enough to kill two of the goat headed men outright. Instead of launching me straight up, this time the thunder clap sent me into a controlled leap up into the air and forward over the line of advancing Spawn. The spell gave me enough control that I could alter my trajectory a bit so that I landed amidst another group of Spawn. I touched down, and the final effect of the spell was released. The force equal to that of an alchemical explosive shell sent Hornmen and parts of Hornmen flying through the air.

The dragoon troopers could hardly miss the chaos that I and my two friends were sowing in the Hornmen's lines. My ears were still ringing by the aftereffects of my spell, so I couldn't hear their reactions. The flash of their primer powder in their flintlock's pans couldn't be missed.

Being on the wrong side of their carbine discharge, made me decided that I really wanted to get to the dragoon's line as fast as possible. Channeling the magic once again, I called upon the warm but strong winds of a desert storm to lift me, gently this time, off the ground and fly me over to where six of the Dragoons had established an effective skirmish line while the others were getting their horses ready to ride.

As I landed, the troop's sergeant called out, "Storm Crow, I figured it had to be you. No one else could make that much noise."

"You need to get out of here! There's at least a hundred of the Spawn attacking. As well, I have two friends out there, and while I don't think a single musket ball would kill them, they probably hold a grudge against the one who shot them," I said in a stumbling report.

The sergeant only nodded and then sent word down the line to make sure they only shot things that had horns; returning his attention back to me he said, "Retreating was already our plan, but thanks for the additional information."

The discussion now done the sergeant finished reloading his carbine and raised it to fire.

I reframed adding any of my own spells to the troop's defence as I've said before, my magic and gunpowder does not mix. Instead I moved back toward the horses and grabbed up saddles and tack for two of the replacement horses so that Miri, Gregor and I would have something to ride. The bearshirt needed his own mount, but Miri and I were light enough that we could share a horse and not tire him excessively.

I was almost finished one when Riley landed back near me again.

"Miri is almost here and Gregor isn't far behind. I'll say this for the bearshirt; he can fight," he said with admiration.

"I was about to answer when a large bulled headed Spawn charged into the midst of the horses. Over three metres tall and armed with a battle ax sized cleaver in each hand; the Minotaur attacked so fast that it cut down both a horse and its handler before either could cry a warning.

Without thinking I called up a powerful bolt of lightning and struck the Spawn square in the chest with enough power to cause him to stagger. I of course regretted my action immediately as the pain of the backlash hit. I'd been so startled by the attack that I had countered the creature without even bothering to draw Lightning, and gotten a painful reminder as to why that was a bad idea. Drawing both of my foci I got ready to face the creature properly.

"Get the horses to the rest of the squad. We're surrounded and going to have to fight our way out," I shouted at the other handlers. "I'll deal with this big bastard."

I was amazed how confident I sounded given how scared I felt. Hornmen coming from this direction meant that either this warband was moving far faster than we first

163

thought or that there were a lot more of them then we'd figured. That was something that we would have to find out, but in the meantime, the creature had recovered from my lightning bolt and I realized that I'd done enough damage to get noticed but not enough for it to fear me. It bellowed in anger and charged towards me, clearly intending to just run me over as it headed towards the skirmish line.

Only I didn't intend to wait for it to run me over.

Channeling my magic through my body, I transformed my physical self once again into a bolt of electrical energy. I then hurled myself at the monster passing through him to become Sasha again behind the creature. Bellowing in pain, the creature appeared to not realize that I was no longer in front of him as he continued charging in the same direction as before. That was fine with me as I caused a blast of wind to hammer into the Spawn from behind. The solid wall of air hit the creature in his knees (which in this case were oriented like a normal human) causing him to pitch forward into the ground his momentum sliding him forward another metre.

I was so pleased with myself that I barely heard Riley's warning. I managed to duck just as a spiked club was suddenly swung at the level where my head had been. I didn't get away clean though; several of the spikes tore off my tricorne, and opened up my scalp and knocked me to the ground. Through the pain and blood, I saw another Hornman, a normal two metre sheep headed one, winding up with his club to finish the job that he'd started on my head. Of course, the Minotaur had brought friends.

But then so had I.

With a banshee scream; Miri leaped onto the club wielding Spawn. Legs wrapped around his middle the Daywalker repeatedly plunged her short sword and dagger into the creature. The Spawn's legs buckled under the assault and he fell backwards onto the snow-covered

164

ground Miri riding him all the way. Then while the beastman still drew breath Miri plunged her fangs in to the creature's neck and started to feed.

I wish I could say that my lover's behavior surprised me. But I'd seen it too often. In fights whose length are measured in minutes instead of seconds; more and more of Miri's vampire heritage came to the fore. She acts the way they always act like; apex predators who fear no mortal creature.

"Sasha! Remember that really big Hornman!" shouted Riley reminding me that I had other concerns at the moment other than my lover overindulging her dark side.

I wobbly got back onto my feet, and looked back towards where my original opponent had been. He was there and standing but only just. My spells had alerted the dragoons to the new threat and the horse handlers had filled the creature with lead bullets from their pistols and carbines. The creature was done for, but his will was such that he refused to die. Letting out a frothy red bellow the Minotaur leveled his head and charged the largest group of dragoons.

He got maybe two metres before Miri, in a blur of movement, struck again. Slashing through the bull man's left knee so deep she almost amputated it. Hamstrung the huge Hornman fell forward his body's momentum creating another furrow in the loose dirt and snow of the field. The dragoons decided to make sure he was going to stay down by putting another volley into the body.

Seeing that creature was dead I turned and looked for more opponents. I didn't see any, instead I got a hard kiss on the lips as Miri just 'appeared' in front of me.

"You smell delicious," she said as she then started to lick my blood from the side of my face.

I say start because an instant later she was on the ground. Her greatcoat scored black where I had pressed lightning into her side and sent a large charge of electricity into her.

"I. Am. Not. Food!" I hissed at Miri. "Now get your longsword and get back here. We're going to act as a battering ram to get the dragoons out of here! Clear?" I ordered her.

The literal shock I'd just given her system was enough to allow Miri to get some control over her darker half. The fangs retracted and her red eyes returned to their normal black colour. "Sasha, I," she started to say.

"Apology accepted. Now move!" I said as I took out a cloth and after wiping the blood from my eyes held it to my bleeding scalp. Looking around I saw my tricorne grabbed it up and jammed it firmly on my head to hold the cloth in place.

By the time I was done Miri got up disappeared back into the night and returned with her magical longsword in hand and still a bit shamefaced.

Looking around I realized that despite the fight that had just occurred around them the two horses that I'd readied were still close at hand and surprisingly calm. Taking up their reins I moved quickly towards where the dragoons were forming up to ride out of here.

At the centre of their position Gregor gleefully reloaded his blunderbuss firing the weapon at any group of Titan Spawn that looked like they had the courage to charge the dragoons. He had reverted back to his largely human shape, only with a more hair than he normally had.

When he saw us coming towards him he shouted "Ha! This is a really good fight!"

Pointing at one of the horses, I shouted back "take it the dragoons are going to need us to punch a hole out of here."

Without say a further word, Gregor got up onto the horse and got ready to act as a bearshirt battering ram.

166

Chapter 11

Despite our best efforts, we had lost half of the dragoons in the skirmish with the Hornmen's warband. But that wasn't the worst part of the night. The boundary between the woods and farmland within Ulm was aflame. The light of the fires and the smoke they produced combined with the fresh snow on the ground to create a truly other worldly environment that made me wonder if it looked more like the Fey or Shadow Reich. It also created enough light for those of us without night sight to actually see where we going.

Through the smoke and snow, we heard a ragged volley of musket fire every so often, but far more often though we heard the savage roars of Hornmen victory cries and the dancing shapes of Spawn backlit by the fires that they had set.

"This is a full-on attack, not just a raid," I said to the dragoon's commanding sergeant as we trotted south.

"Agreed; I suggest that we head east across country and try to get around them instead of riding south into them," he said.

"You get no argument from me," I replied.

With a sharp whistle and hand gesture the sergeant got the remaining dragoons heading east. After two hours of riding we all dismounted and walked our mounts. We had been lucky so far and had lost only two horses to rabbit holes, but all the animals were showing signs of fatigue: having been ridden for most of the day and now the night.

By this time Miri was fully in control of her vampiric aspect but she couldn't look me in the eye. She'd come close to breaking one of our fundamental rules and didn't know what to say to make it better. Given my own mood right then, that was likely a good thing. My scalp wound had stopped bleeding and now felt like a burning brand on the side of my head. This combined with the blood loss, the fatigue from a short heavy use of my magic, and not eating for close to twenty hours, had left me in too much pain, and too light headed to be fully in control of my emotions. At least the slower walking pace allowed Gregor and me to wolf down some dried fruit, trail bread and a small wheel of cheese; all washed down by a bottle of local white wine which I cut with a lot of water. Miri had gallantly offered to lead our horses so that Gregor and I could eat with both of our hands.

After half an hour walking, we were back in the saddle and making our way south west back towards the Prince's keep and our base. We were perhaps an hour out from camp when we finally ran into some good fortune, in the form of a patrol of our Hobgoblin scouts.

We stopped and let the patrol ride towards us.

"Greetings my friends you are a welcome sight. We've ridden since the first signs of attack. You have been the only members of the Company that we've come across. So far this appears to be the main hoard and the Captain is moving to intercept them as far away from the keep and the bulk of the population as possible," said the leader of the scouts. Like all of his brethren, the Hobgoblin was dressed in a dark green and yellow Hussar uniform. The only differences were the layered steel scales sown into the fabric of his tunic and coat where I had the thick silk lace. Like his other scouts he was heavily armed: with a lance, both curved and straight swords, a brace of heavy horse pistols and a powerful composite horse bow. He sat hunched over his large wolf his eyes always moving and an indifferent sneer on his face that reminded me more of his steppe raiding ancestors, than the members of the Imperium that they really were.

"Where's the Captain now?" I asked in accented Goblin.

"He's with the vanguard, of course, Storm Crow. He'll

be glad to see you. As far as I know you and these men are the only sellswords that have made it back from the northern tripwire," replied the Hobgoblin.

"Where is the vanguard roughly now?" I asked.

The scout pointed almost directly due west and said "Head that way and you should hit it in an hour of hard riding, two if you don't want to risk killing your mounts."

"Or half an hour as the raven flies," I said glancing to Riley.

"Oh no," replied the familiar. "I left your side once and you nearly killed yourself. I'm not making that mistake again."

"It's probably wise that he stays with you anyways. We've seen bats and Harpies flying to the south," said the Hobgoblin.

"Right I'm staying right here on your shoulder where it's reasonably safe," replied Riley. Okay he had a point this time. The large flesh and blood eating bats were bad enough. But the Harpies were a whole different world of bad. The only Spawn that outwardly had female attributes, these flying creatures were the main reason why so many sellswords still carried blunderbusses.

"Okay fine," I said to the bird. Turning to the dragoon sergeant I said, "We need to get to Roland as soon as possible. Miri, Gregor and I will be heading west. Given where we are I know where Roland is going to make his stand. I'm not expecting you to join us but I'll need your horses until then.

It was dangerous and the dragoons had already done their piece. They could have easily left it up to us to report to Roland and head to the rear to join up with the main Dragoon body. But the sergeant stepped up.

"We'll see this to the end," he said,

With a nod to the scouts we turned and started hopefully our final ride of the night.

Chapter 12

I consider it a sign of my growing understanding of how to fight a battle, that when we made contact with Roland and the rest of the Company it was where I expected them to be. I had been with Roland when he had surveyed the terrain within the Principality, and I knew that a small crest ran between Ulm's keep and the northern lands. It was maybe five metres higher than the land around it; hardly anything more than a gentle slope. But it blocked line of site behind it and increased it to the front; and given the way that Roland intended to fight this battle this advantage was worth getting.

The first light of dawn was breaking as we rode up towards the crest. I saw that Roland was already there with the Company's vanguard. The bulk of the dragoons had setup a picket line on the crest that had been strengthen by the Company's Anglo warbowmen. In front of the picket line I saw fifty or so goat and sheep headed Spawn dead; each sporting one or two bullet holes or five or more broadhead arrows. Perhaps half a kilometre past their dead brethren stood a growing swarm of Titan Spawn screaming and braying their displeasure at our presence. Roland had succeeded in getting his choice of battle ground but it had been close.

On the other side of the crest I saw the rest of the Company, reading for battle, slogging to the position. The snow wasn't that deep yet, perhaps twenty centimetres, but it was wet and had compacted into either ice or mush quickly. Already the monster killer, heavy infantry, struggled under the weight of their arms and armour. While on their flanks rode the cuirassiers, their heavy horses kicking up mud. Whatever else this battle was going to be today it was going to be messy.

"Sasha!"

Roland's bellow broke me out of my momentary

stupor and I nudged my horse towards our Captain.

"Well you three are an unexpected sight. I had feared that you were lost," said the Golem. He was next to a small map table surrounded by his staff, Keira and several other Sellswords which served as his personal guard.

"We were lucky," I replied as I gratefully accepted a mug of coffee that Keira had thoughtfully reheated with a minor spell. Seeing the bloody half of my face, the book mage clucked in disapproval, got me to sit down so that she could get a better look at the injury. It felt unusual giving my report while sitting down but no one dared to say a word while the book mage worked.

Roland and his staff listened attentively, only interrupting to have me point things out on the map. I've done this sort of report for Roland before so I had a pretty good idea of what to both include and not include. When I was done, Roland turned to his staff and asked their opinions.

"The Storm Crow report agrees with your assessment Captain. This is a big push on the Spawns part. However, whether it's the big push remains to be seen. Either way there are too many of the beasts to ignore. Your plan seems best given the circumstances," said a Grizzled Human name Claz. He had a beard and build that Gregor would have been proud of.

The other staff officers just nodded their heads in agreement. They appeared to be confident but not cocky. They knew from hard experience that no plan survived contact with the enemy, but they also knew that the maxim also applied to the enemy. The key to victory was to make the enemies' plan unravel first.

"Alight everyone knows the plan. Rejoin your commands; the Spawn may hit us at any time. The Princess is mobilizing her forces for defending the keep and the surrounding territory, but they will not be needed," said Roland to his officers as they were getting ready to leave.

171

"Princess?" I asked Keira quietly.

"Oh right; you were already out on your long-range patrol weren't you. The Prince died two days ago. His daughter has taken over unofficially for now, her coronation will have to wait until the Principality is safe," whispered the book mage as she got me to forward again. She had deadened the area and up till then I hadn't realized that she'd been stitching the cut close while I was actually giving my report.

Roland needlessly cleared his throat to get my and Keira's attention. "I apologize for interrupting your gossiping ladies, but we still have the minor problem of an upcoming battle that we need to deal with before we can move onto local politics. Sasha, I know you three must be exhausted, but I need you with the other Soldants over there," he said as he pointed towards a large manor house and what was the anchor for our left flank.

"All of the cuirassiers will be deploying behind the crest near the manor. It is absolutely vital that they are ready to charge when I need them to charge. I've put Sariel in command of the soldants and she'll need your help to keep the Spawn off the cavalry until then," he said finally.

"I've stitched the wound closed; the healing salve I used is one that I created specifically for head wounds. Along with accelerating healing it also encourages hair growth. No one will even know that you have a scar," said Keira reassuringly.

I gave her a 'thank you' smile then turned and looked behind the mainline to where the company cooks had already setup their elemental stoves and were busy cooking up a lot of hot food.

"Could we grab a hot meal first Captain?" I asked.

The Golem nodded "It's the least that you deserve, given what you've just been through."

"It is much nicer to fight on a full stomach," agreed Gregor.

172

Chapter 13

After wolfing down our first hot meal of the day, the three of us moved towards the manor house that we were supposed to help defend. As defensive positions go it could have been worse. The noble whose home it was must have had enough pull with the prince so that he didn't have to destroy it or the outer buildings. Constructed from thick worked stone, the two-storied building was rectangular in shape with its one hundred metre length serving as an anchor point for the two-metre-tall wall that enclosed the rest of the manor's buildings, which like the main house were made out of stone. As a whole, it was clear that the manor had been built in a time when attacks from rivals must not have been unheard of. All in all, it was a reasonable defensive position, and our arrived couldn't have been timed better. For just as we climbed over the manor wall, the gates had long been sealed, we heard the sound of several hundred horns announcing the first charge of the Titan Spawn towards our lines.

Bestial they may be, the Spawn's leaders were no fool. Five hundred metres was a lot space and even in idea conditions would have taken over ninety seconds to cover at a full run. Given the snow and mud it was going to take over twice that time. Even fit troops would be spent if they tried to run that distance. Instead he somehow managed to control the horde's speed to a fast walk, with them braying out what I thought were insults as they smashed their weapons against shields.

"Noisy group, aren't they?" I heard one soldant say nearby.

"Once they're less than a hundred metres we'll drown them out," I said with confidence.

"We'll start sooner than that," said Sariel walking up with the confidence of a veteran officer, her black great coat and tricorne making her stand out as much as any other uniform. Like those she supposedly 'commanded' she had chosen not to dress in the Hussar uniform that she herself had designed.

"How did you end up in command?" Miri asked, voicing my own questions for the Fey.

"The Captain felt that I had the proper attitude to command the soldants in a battle. By the way no one but the snipers are supposed to shoot until the manor itself is under direct attack. If the Spawn ignore us so much the better," replied Sariel with a serious expression on her face. While it looked right now, I just could not place upon the woman that I had rescued two months ago.

"Don't think about it too much Sasha. The Fey are mercurial creatures who literally change their character to fit the role they perceive that others want them to play," whispered Riley.

Sariel was about to give Riley a sharp retort but was interrupted by the sharp crash of our four-alchemical cannon as they opened fire. All of our attention was turned back towards the Titan Spawn's advancing line as four intense fireballs maybe five metres across struck the lines sending Hornmen flying into the air while others became burning pyres of screaming flesh. The cannon were an amazing mixture of magic and alchemy. Gunpowder propelled enchanted shot that, depending upon the enchantment, either exploded into a fireball, froze the target under a sheet of solid ice, or caused a lightning bolt to discharge deep into the enemy's ranks. I admit I have a bias but I did feel that this last effect was the most impactful upon the enemy.

"Jorg, Catlin can you make out their leaders and shamans yet?" shouted Sariel to someone in the upper level of a nearby barn.

"I think so Sariel," came a reply from the barn.

"Right start weakening their leadership," Sariel called back. Then turning to me she said with a wink "kill the

175

mages, first, right?"

My reply was interrupted by the crack of Jorg's jaeger rifle, a slow loading musket that made up for this deficit by its accuracy over long ranges. Catlin was another soldant sniper. Her weapon of preference was a powerful two-metre-long war bow with which she was even more accurate than Jorg was with his rifle.

I returned my gaze back to the Spawn attack and noticed something that made my heart miss several beats. While the front line of the Spawn closed to three hundred metres of our lines, there were still more coming into view.

"How many of them are there?" I breathed.

"As far as we know: between three to four thousand," said Sariel calmly.

"So best case we're outnumbered three to one?" I asked.

"Yes, but that doesn't take into account how many Minotaurs that they may have or how powerful their battlefield magic is," continued the Fey

"So, it was to be one of those fights," I said: discipline and firepower versus savagery and a willingness to take casualties. Miri and I had cut our teeth on those kind of battles, the first time we'd fought with Roland against the Phoenix Republic's undead legions. We had won several battles but lost the one that had mattered. We'd been lucky to survive that fight and learn the lessons from it.

I looked over at Miri and I saw the same fear in her eyes as I felt. Suddenly we both started to speak at the same time. We both paused and I let Miri speak first.

"Sasha, I have to know that you forgive me for what happened. I lost control. You were absolutely right in what you did... Please don't hate me for breaking our trust,"

She probably had more to say but I didn't care. I leaned forward and kissed her hard, making any further apology moot.

Sometimes actions spoke louder than words.

"Do you city folk always act like it's time to say goodbye before a fight?" asked Gregor confused.

"They're scared Gregor, the last time we faced this kind of fight...it didn't come out well," explained Riley.

"But that was last time, not now. You're stronger now and I am here. I came here to kill Titan Spawn, not to die," he said to all three of us brightly.

"Well said Gregor," said Sariel who turned to Miri and I and added. "I'm in charge here and I order you not to die."

With that she turned on her heel like a proper officer and started to walk down the wall shouting encouragement and profanity to other soldants in equal measure.

"Well I guess that tears it; we can't die unless we want to be charged with disobeying orders," I said to Miri.

Miri just nodded in agreement as she pulled out her Hobgoblin composite bow and got ready for the order to fire.

We didn't have to wait long. As the Spawn closed to within two hundred metres of our lines the Anglo archers started to loose volley after volley of metre long broad head arrows at the horde. In response, they sped up their attack from a fast walk to an outright charge.

The alchemical cannons each got one more round off before the enemy closed to one hundred metres in distance. This was a freezing shot and forty metres of the advancing horde was suddenly halted under thick ice. The front ranks of the horde were thrown into confusion as half of them slammed into their frozen comrades while the other half advanced with large gaps in their lines. Into this confusion our musketeers started to fire.

Firing by platoons of twenty-five the Company's line rippled in a continual line of fire down its length as their first volley was fired. The impact of the volley was horrific upon the Titan Spawn. The ice covered Hornmen were cut down, as muskets balls shattered ice and bone with equal efficiency. The first two ranks of the other Beastmen just disappeared as platoon after platoon of fire tore into them. The Horde stumbled and monetarily slowed they're charge, as if they were a single great beast hit by massive blow. This allowed our battle line to fire another rippling volley into the horde; adding to its confusion and the general chaos.

While bloodied the Titan Spawn horde was still far from defeated, nor were they without tricks of their own. My skin crawled and I suddenly felt nauseous as Titan magic even more corrupted than what the druid had used started to form at the centre of our lines. At the exact same time, I heard the screech of hundreds of winged harpies; screaming their hate as they dove out of the morning sun and onto the alchemical cannons.

But Roland was ready with counter measures for these attacks. Or more to the point Keira was ready. Just before the spell erupted into a cloud of poisonous gas that would have killed hundreds, the book mage drained the area of magic starving the attacking spell of the vital energy it needed to fully manifest. The first twenty harpies which attacked the cannons were turned to ash as the defensive runes that the artillerymen had drawn around their positions were activated by the commander of the battery.

Then a ragged volley from the remaining Dragoons tore into the flying Spawn before they charged into the flock with curved swords and flintlock pistols at the ready.

But the attacks still had an impact. Enough of the poison cloud spell manifested to cause coughing fits in two of the Companies central platoons, preventing them from firing a third volley. The Harpies, who were dying in droves still kept the cannons from firing their third volley as well. Not to mention that they were killing or wounding many of the cannon's crewmen so if they did manage to drive the Harpies off I doubted that they'd be able to get all four cannons back into action.

178

Still we were inflicting heavy losses upon the horde, and they hadn't managed to hit our front lines yet, so was I still hopeful. That was until a second set of Beastmen horns sounded and two hundred or so Minotaurs stood up and charged followed by the largest and best equipped Hornmen.

"That was different," said Gregor surprised. "Usually they are pushing each other out of the way to get to the enemy. Their warboss must be really smart, and scary for them to act with any discipline."

As much as I didn't want to, I had to agree with the bearshirt. This wasn't the mindless mob of Titan Spawn that at least I had been expecting; I hoped Roland was up for the challenge.

It was then that I heard his augmented voice once again blare out over the battlefield. "At them you whoresons! Show them your steel!"

With that the monster hunters moved through the musketeer ranks and counter charged the Minotaurs, Roland at their head. Behind them the musketeers started to fire at will, aiming their shots to take down individual targets.

And this was pretty much all of the main battle I was able to witness for as the horde hit our main line of defence it started to spread out. Then every soldant in the manor house saw a solid block of about a hundred Gnolls heading towards us. As expected their elite was trying to outflank the ridge and we were right in their way.

Chapter 14

"Shoot the Gnolls!" shouted Sariel at the top of her lungs as they approached our lines.

At the Fey's 'suggestion' all twenty of the soldants let loose with some sort of missile attack. Arrows, bullets, both from muskets and slings, and several spells were directed towards the canine headed Spawn. What the soldant's lacked in volume of fire we more than made up for with the skill that were used to execute those attacks. Ten Gnoll's went down with our first volley and we got two more volleys off before the Gnolls had closed to melee range.

Just before they hit, I released as large an explosion of wind and thunder as I could manage. I'd been fighting, casting or running steady for over twelve hours now, but I tried to put as much into the spell as I could. Breaking the Gnoll's charge momentum right now was going to be our best chance of winning this fight with as few casualties as possible.

Maybe thirty of the Gnolls on the front line were staggered enough by the wind that the Gnolls behind them slamed into them; causing what could best be described as a jumble of Gnolls.

Gregor and a few others had been waiting just for this situation and several shot their blunderbusses at the tightly packed target. Two others threw grenades letting jagged pieces of iron rip through the living wall. To add more insult to that injury Sariel threw a flask of burning oil into the mix.

"Sariel! Really!" shouted Miri indignantly.

"What? Isn't burning oil the traditional weapon of soldants?" was our supposed commander's reply.

Miri didn't bother with a reply because right then what remained of the Gnoll's attack hit the wall, and the real battle began.

The soldant didn't fight in anything close to what could be called a formation, but we had fought several mock battles against the Prince's melee troops to get a better idea of what each of us were capable of. So our defence wasn't so much the tight mechanical battle line that the rest of the Company had just displayed but a series of individuals and small groups tied together in cooperative self-interest.

Miri and Gregor hacked and cleaved their way through several Gnolls, neither bothered to watch their backs expecting me and Riley to have enough awareness of the fight to keep them safe. Fortunately thanks to Thunder and Lightning, I was able to maintain enough attacks that I was actually able keep up on my end of that bargain.

At least I was able to keep up until the Gnoll's own soldants started to make their presence known. All at once, the cement that held the stones together along the ten-metre section of the wall that we were fighting behind started to smoke and turn a sickly shade of green. Seconds later the stone wall just exploded inward, sending jagged shards of stone into both Gnoll and mortal who had been fighting there. I was far enough back that I was able to keep my footing but several stone shards hit me and I felt sharp pains in both my left arm and leg, as something tore through my leather great coat.

Through the breech walked one of the Gnoll's Titan Shamans. What was most scary about him was just how small he was. If he stood on his tip toes he may have reached two metres in height. For a Gnoll that small to have survived, let alone achieve a position of power, within the herd; spoke of a very dangerous monster indeed.

He was also surprisingly the best groomed Gnoll I have ever faced. His black tightly curled hair showed no sign of the usual mange of his brethren; in fact, it looked combed. Even his armour and spear, though obviously

Gnoll in manufacture, were clean and rust free. Replacing the grime and rust was a sickly green energy that flicked around the metal of both items. I felt the magic change as the energy focused into a green liquid that covered the spear's large serrated head.

As he walked through the hole in the wall that he'd just created, he arrogantly scanned the battle looking for new opponents. Seeing me he said one word "Maaaaage."

As I brought up Thunder and Lightning to face him, my mind raced through the spells that I knew and compared them to the energy that I had left in me; and came up with scarily few options. I chose the best option and raising Thunder, I slashed down with the blade, releasing a thunderous blast of wind in the hopes that I could at least blow him out of the compound.

Only as the wind hit him he swept up his spear and ate the spell's magic. To make matters worse some of the green liquid flew off the spearhead and where it landed sizzle black smoke rose.

"Oh, this just keeps getting better and better," said Riley.

Fortunately, that was when Miri attacked. Other than me, Miri was the only being that stayed upright after the explosion. Knowing that I was going to attack, she did what we'd long ago worked out as our attack plan in these situations: wait and attack the now 'weakened' enemy to finish it off.

Only this enemy was still at the heights of it power and more than capable of taking her on. With a blur the Gnoll shaman turned and brought his spear up and parried, much to Miri surprise, the downward strike, she had aimed at his head.

With a snarl the Gnoll swung the butt of the spear low in an attempt to take out Miri's legs, but he only got air as she back flipped out of the spear's reach.

The two combatants eyed each other with a sudden

wariness. Both the Gnoll and Miri relied on their speed and agility as their major assets in combat. For perhaps the first time, each of them faced an opponent who matched them in that capacity. Now as a score of Gnolls and perhaps five soldants raced for control of the breach a very private duel took place.

It lasted only seconds and I wish I could describe it with any great detail but even to my combat heightened senses it looked to be only a blur of movement; that ended with Miri being hoisted up upon the Shaman's spear two metres into the air, the serrated blade a full ten centimeters past her back.

I'm afraid to admit that I was stunned into inaction. I had been so confident of Miri's skills and abilities that it never entered my mind that she could have been defeated.

The Gnoll screamed in triumphant rage and after showing off his new battle banner, he attempted to drive the spear down into the ground so that he could saw out the spearhead from Miri's still twitching body. Only Miri had other ideas. Once again, her Vampire heritage came to the fore. I watched in amazement as Miri gave an equally violent scream as she pulled herself down the spear's shaft leaving parts of her intestines along the sides of the rough wood, and transfix the Gnoll's chest upon her longsword's magic blade.

They then just stood there. Transfixed; staring at each other in death's embrace; neither willing to give the other the satisfaction of dying first. The noise of their combine screams had caused the entire fight around the breech to pause as everyone, Spawn and mortal alike turned to look towards the final death throes of what appeared to have been a climactic duel.

Which is when Gregor stepped up and cut the Gnoll's head from his body with a single swing of his ax.

With a snort of disgust the bearshirt grabbed up the severed Shaman's head and holding it before the Gnoll's screamed at them in their guttural excuse of a language. This was apparently enough for the Titan Spawn and they started to retreat from the wall.

Just as the Gnolls broke, we heard Roland's amplified voice boom out across the battlefield with a single word, "Hammer!"

With that all of our Cuirassier heavy cavalry moved from their hidden positions. At the run they moved past the Spawn's flanks reformed quickly into two ranks and struck the rear of the engaged Horde at a full gallop. The big armoured mortals on heavy warhorses hit the Spawn rear like a rock hits a pane of glass, shattering it under the charge. Hornmen were thrown into the air and trampled to pieces as the cavalry horses clove deeper into the horde.

The unexpected attack to their rear was enough for most of the Titan Spawn. They broke off their attack and in draggled groups both large and small they started to rout from the field.

We'd done it. We'd routed the Titan Spawn and gave them a solid bloody nose. And as I finally broke from my trance, and ran to Miri I couldn't have cared less.

Chapter 15

As I approached Miri I said to Riley, "Go and get Keira; either get her here or one of her infusions or potions and get back here as quickly as possible.

"Sasha: she's been eviscerated. There are some wounds even a potion can't," I didn't let him finish.

"Miri fed heavily last night! We've both seen a Vampire recover from far worst wounds. Now stop arguing and GO GET KEIRA!" I screamed like an overwrought Banshee.

Wisely the Raven just took flight without saying another word, as I knelt beside Miri. Gregor was still there and cradled my love in his arms as gently as a newborn. She was still conscious but was mumbling incoherently in pain.

"Will my blood help?" he asked with a helpless earnestly. His big eyes full of worry and tears.

I shook my head, "She fed last night. She's already at the peak of her vampiric strength." I said as I opened her greatcoat and shirt.

I then involuntary pulled away; and took several deep breaths so as to not get sick from sight and smell that revealed itself. The spear had struck Miri at the top of her stomach and its serrated head had proceeded to saw its way through her stomach and intestines and then through her back. That it had missed both the spine and diaphragm were the only reasons why Miri had been able to deliver her counter blow.

There was so much blood: and bile and shit and piss and whatever else there is inside a person's guts. As I had said the smell was overwhelming. But my arcane senses also picked up on something else: the sickly oversweet smell of necromantic magic that was at the heart of Vampiric power. I had been right; Miri's body was trying to regenerate itself.

185

"We have to get this spear out of her! Its preventing her from healing the same way a stake prevents a full vampire from coming back to life," I said to Gregor.

"Really? The storytellers got that one, right?" asked Gregor surprise in his voice.

I didn't bother replying trying to figure out how best to get Miri off a spear that she was almost in the direct middle of. Pulling it through her seemed the best idea but one end had the spear head and the other end was shod in steel.

"Tilt her back so that as much of the head is touching the ground as possible. And whatever you do don't touch me or the spear for the next few seconds," I told Gregor. I then grabbed the spear with both hands behind her back and started to channel as much electrical energy as possible into the spear.

Electricity really is marvellous. All it wants to do is to ground itself into the earth by the easiest path possible. What it considers the easiest path can sometimes be a mystery to an outside observer; but if you know that basic rule you can get it to do some pretty impressive things. Like now where I channeled every ounce of electrical energy down to the metal spearhead and back into the ground. Almost immediately the spear shaft started to blacken and smoke. It then started to crack and finally disintegrated into a line of white ash.

Without even thinking I moved to the other side of Miri's body and pulled the remains of the spear shaft from her, allowing her vampiric half to start working to keep her alive.

Having accomplished that goal, my mind finally allowed my body to register that it was not happy with me, and that I'd done something that Riley was going to get mad at me about again.

Normally I channel short blasts of lightning into my bolts, factions of seconds at most. I had just continually channeled that same level of energy into my body and

186

through my hands for several seconds. My hands were rapidly swelling with massive burn blisters. My natural resistance to electricity most likely prevented the flesh from frying off to the bone, but given the pain I was in right then I didn't really care.

I managed not to scream as I desperately tried to open my bag of holding to get something out of it that would help Miri or reduce my own pain. Unfortunately, the shock that my mind was in wouldn't allow me to work the magical command to open the thing.

Then Gregor was beside me pouring the remains of the watered wine onto my hands.

"You just can't stop being stupid when people in danger can you?" he chided.

I was about to say something when I felt the magical presence of a Fey arriving.

"It's a damn good thing that the Spawn are in retreat because you just flared with so much magic that even I felt it," said Sariel crossly as she tossed Gregor a potion bottle, and started to pour the contents of a second down Miri's throat.

"I picked these up in Flores, nowhere near as good as Keira's but they'll do for now," she said with a note of annoyance. Her black clothing was shiny with what appeared to be other peoples blood, but she'd lost her hat somewhere in the fight and her blonde hair now had several long streaks of blood in it.

As Gregor opened the bottle and helped me drink it down I quickly started to feel better but was still exhausted to the point that all that was keeping me moving was the anxiety over Miri.

Seeing that we'd taken in the healing potions, Sariel rose and shifted once again from annoyed friend to commanding officer.

"We've won the battle but there's a chance to win the war as well. Roland wants to pursue the Spawn back to the forest killing as many of the stragglers as possible to make the point that Ulm is not an easy target and they should look elsewhere for their winter stores. Once help for these two arrive we need your help fighting the remaining pockets.

Gregor nodded in understanding.

Sariel then took off shouting command to the other soldants to advance. I hate to admit it but it surprised me to see the other, normally anti-authoritarian sorts actually follow her. I swear that Fey had more masks than an entire theatre troop.

With the pain of my hands reduced I was able to dig out a clean shirt and then a bedroll from my bag of holding and used them to cover Miri so that I no longer had a ringside seat to how a healing potion combined with vampire magic 'realigned' someone's intestines.

"Gregor, go. I know you hate feeling helpless and there's really nothing else that you can do to help right now," I said to the bearshirt.

Gregor looked like he was going to stay but then he unslung his blunderbuss reloaded the weapon with what looked to be a double load of shot, and then handed it to me. "Looks like you're out of magic. If a spawn attacks pull back hammer, wait till he's really close and pull the trigger: it will cut him in half. And with that he grabbed up his ax and moved once again back into the fight.

I gave him a tired smile. The pagan bearshirt had really turned out to be a good friend. I felt a bit silly holding the blunderbuss, but I kept watch over what now appeared to be a battlefield only inhabited by corpses until Riley flew back onto my shoulder.

"The ambulance is on its way. Keira has her hands too full at the field hospital to leave. And what exactly did you do to flare like you did?" he said.

I was going to answer him, but upon seeing the ambulance coming towards us, I felt myself slipping into unconsciousness.

Chapter 15

I awoke at the field hospital propped up on a chair next to the cot where Miri lay. Judging by the light, I guessed that it was near noon. Had the battle only lasted the morning? It felt like we'd been fighting for days.

I tried to shift my position but the attempt had been the permission that my body had been waiting for to let me know just how much it hadn't like how I'd been treating it the past twenty-four hours.

The groan had been enough to let Riley know that I was awake. "Afternoon sunshine; did you enjoy your little nap?" he asked in a smug tone.

I didn't bother answering; instead I looked over to where Miri lay. She was sleeping, but not comfortably. She was pale even for her, and her blankets were damp with sweat. One of Keira's infusions was flowing into her arm and I no longer sensed the vampiric magic working the way that it had earlier.

"Keira induced her into a deep sleep. Unfortunately, Sariel's healing potion did more harm than good. Keira had to purge her system before she could introduce something more effective. Even with that Miri isn't responding as well as Keira expected," said Riley reading my thoughts.

"Why did the healing potion hurt?" I asked.

"The vampiric portion of Miri's body was still in full control at the time. Necromantic healing doesn't combine well with cheap healing magic meant for a completely mortal being. Don't blame Sariel, Keira said she would have done the same thing in a battlefield situation," replied Riley.

"Will she be alright?" I asked taking Miri's hand into mine. It was then that I noticed that my hands had been lightly bandaged.

"I'm honestly not sure. Riley said that the spear that ripped her open was covered by a magical green liquid," said Keira as she moved next to me. "That liquid seems to be preventing the regeneration that should have occurred by both Miri's magic and the new infusions that I've introduced. I manually reconnected as many of the major organs as possible, but the damage to the intestines was just too severe for me to get everything,"

The book mage appeared to have as much energy as she ever did, but the dark bags under her eyes made me wonder just how much willpower she was running on.

"As for you: your system has taken in as much magical healing as it can in one day. You're going to have to wait a day or two before we can get your physical injuries healed. However, for now drink this," she said as she handed me a flask of watered wine.

I was barely able to say thank you before Keira left us and moved on to another wounded member of the Company. Looking around it finally became apparent to me that we were both in the Company's Hospital tent. An example of the Old Empire's capacity for magic, on a command word the tent expanded by itself and provided a clean operating room and a recovery ward with fifty cots. Another command word would cause it to clean itself and fold back down into a bundle small enough for a single mule to carry it.

"How did the battle go?" I asked Riley.

"From what I've seen here and what I overheard from Roland we won but it's a high bill. Around a hundred dead outright, and maybe two hundred wounded. Keira is going be able to keep most of those alive but a hundred or so won't be able to fight again. Spawn cleavers are just too effective in removing limbs for it to be otherwise.

"Keira pulled a Keira and just by looking at the battlefield estimated that we killed or wounded, two thousand Titan Spawn. The cavalry is pursuing the Spawn, making sure that they keep heading back to the forest and will most likely account for several hundred more," said

Riley finishing his report.

I sighed in relief, Riley was right it was a high price but it would have been far higher if the Company hadn't been here. The image of those children I'd met in the keep and knowing that they'd be alive tomorrow was something I took comfort in right then.

"Sasha," called out someone from the other side of the tent.

Riley and I turned around to see Sariel enter the tent. Then I felt gut punched as I saw that she was carrying Gregor's ax in her blood covered hands: her face a mask of sorrow mixed with guilt.

"It was the craziest accident. The cannon had stopped firing magic shot but were still firing iron balls. One of the shots must have struck a rock and deflected or something because they weren't firing anywhere near where he was," Sariel paused for a second.

"But he's a bearshirt he can regenerate," I started not wanting to believe what Sariel was telling me.

"Sasha, the shot took his head completely off, there's no coming back from that. I'm sorry Gregor's dead," said the Fey.

I collapsed back down onto the chair, missed and ended up on the tent floor next to Miri's cot; very much just wanting this day to end.

Chapter 17

Because of Miri's wounds, and the fact that I was, at least for the foreseeable future, completely useless as a spellcaster, Keira put us on the first wagon of wounded that were being transported back to our main camp and Ulm's keep. Miri was still unconscious and a fever ravaged her body as it fought to both heal and purge itself of the Shaman's poison. I wasn't in much better shape. Gregor's death had been the straw that broke the camel's back: effectively two days of fighting and heavy spell use, having a fight with the woman I loved, then watching helplessly as she fought for her life and then losing a friend in a completely stupid death. My mind just wanted to shut down for a while.

So, I just sat in the back of the covered wagon, holding Miri's hand in mine. A part of me heard people say things to me, and I felt Riley rub against my cheek every so often. However, acknowledging their words and actions with anything over a single word just seemed like more effort than I wanted to expend right then.

Keira was coming with the convoy of wounded, and it seemed like she was constantly yelling at the drivers of the wagons to be careful and avoid jarring the wagons too much. As a result, we travelled slowly but smoothly. At some point night passed, because when I felt Miri squeeze my hand the eastern sky was starting to glow the orangey red of predawn.

Looking over I saw my lover's eyes were open and she looked at me still in pain but no longer feverish.

"Hi," I said never realizing before just how much you could put into a single word.

"Need to," she started expectantly.

Knowing what she wanted I said "Keira said no blood until her infusions are done working. Her healing will work better without your vampiric aspect trying to undo everything…" I stopped talking as Miri nearly crushed my hand.

"I need to hear you say 'I forgive you: you idiot,'" she whispered.

"Oh: I forgive you, and I love you," were all the words I could say in say.

We passed like that for several seconds. Just holding hands tightly; enjoying the silence together. It was then that I realized that we had stopped moving and that Riley was nowhere to be seen.

The last mystery was solved first when I saw the Raven return; flying into the back of the wagon over the other patients to land near Miri's shoulder.

"Welcome back to the living," he said to Miri. Turning up to me he said "something is going down outside that Keira could use your help with.

"Tell the book mage that I'm not," I started.

"Oh, for fuck sake, Sasha you think for minute that either Keira or I would get you to leave Miri's side if it wasn't for a damn good reason?" my familiar said angerly.

He did have a point, with a sigh I got up slowly, and with a lot more effort than it should have taken for someone in a twenty-year-old body, I managed to get out of the wagon without stepping on anyone else. As I got out of the wagon I saw that Keira had once again made a good decision in calling me; for as I looked down the road I saw Princess Adela at the head of what appeared to be two squadrons of cavalry. The princess was in a black military uniform, I assume to show that she was in mourning, though it was cut to make clear that she was indeed a woman.

Keira being Keira she was ill-equipped to handle the political niceties of dealing with nobles on her best day. Given that she was as exhausted as the rest of us, covered in the blood and grime of keeping good men alive and if I knew her at all, beating herself up about the ones she

194

couldn't save she was hardly at her best. While I wasn't at my best either, my diplomatic skills were probably up to keeping everyone alive in this situation.

I looked down at myself and I realized that I was still wearing the same blouse, and pants that I'd been wearing since before the fight at the Dragoon camp. They stank, were torn, stained with blood dirt and 'other' fluids. Hardly what one should be seen in while talking with royalty, especially when you were not sure of where you stood politically with the new head of state. Fortunately, Riley came to my, rescue as he landed on the edge of the wagon next to me, my bag of holding in his beak.

I quickly reached into it and pulled out a wineskin of rose water and my last clean cloth. As I quickly gave my face and hands a wash, I gave my head a quick flick forward invoking the ritual that I'd learned from Sariel three months ago. Suddenly my hair was clean, brushed and styled into the same low ponytail I'd worn the entire campaign. Putting the cloth and rosewater back into the bag I pulled out the Hussar's dolman jacket I'd worn the first time I was in her presence. My hands had healed enough that I was able to button the jacket up halfway before they started to bleed. Knowing that this was the very best I'd be able to get my appearance, I stepped out from behind the wagon and walked calmly but quickly to where Keira stood.

"Sasha! Thank the Master Wizard and all his journeymen, please talk with her and make her allow us to pass. I need to look in on everyone," Keira said her voice a near panic.

"Miri's awake," I said in a surprisingly calm voice. Suddenly being put into a situation that I felt somewhat competent to handle, actually made me feel better than I had in hours.

"She is! That's good news. I'll look in on her first," said Keira as she had turned around and all but ran back to the wagon that Miri and I had been riding in.

Turning back to the oncoming troops I saw that Princess Adela had a confused look upon her face, not exactly sure as to what was going on. "Citizen Storm Crow how fair you this day?"

"Citizen? Oh, this isn't good," whispered Riley in my ear.

"As well as can be expected your Grace. We fought a battle against the Titan Spawn and drove them from the field, but the victory was paid for in our dearest blood. We are returning to our camp with our most grievously wounded. We are also grieved at hearing of the passage of your father of course," I said keeping things as civil as I could.

"I heard of your victory. The Good Hauptmann asked for our cavalry to aid in keeping the Spawn running, I decided that I should accompany my troops on this campaign. And please there is no need for Your Grace, I am no longer a Princess of an envelope size piece of land, but instead a simple citizen of the great Phoenix Republic," said the young woman in front of me.

"Your Gra...Citizen Adela? When? How did this happen?" I asked with perhaps a more accusatory tone than was safe, given the situation.

"Citizen Stain and I signed the Terms of Unification last night. Already the people of Ulm are receiving the fruits of the Eternal Republic. Within days they will be able to return to their former homes and start to rebuild," said Citizen Adela excitedly.

"I am sure your people will be glad to hear that," I said cautiously.

"Oh, don't worry Citizen Storm Crow I made sure that the contract your Company entered into with my father will be honoured in both the letter and spirit," she said loud enough for everyone in the first couple of wagons to hear.

Citizen Adela then turned to one of the cavalry officers

196

that rode with her. "Citizen Hauptmann please continue forward and provide Hauptmann Roland with whatever aid that you can. I wish to stay here and personally give my thanks to these brave men and women. I will catch up with you, when I've discharged that duty here."

The 'Citizen' Captain followed his orders with obvious signs of relief. Without further command, the cavalry spit into two columns and proceeded to ride past our wagons. Leaving the former Princess with a rather large entourage of couriers and personal guards.

Then one by one each wagon moved forward slowly, allowing Citizen Adela to get on board, where she personally thanked every conscious Sellsword. When done she would jump off the wagon and move onto the next. Along with her came several of her personal bodyguards who appeared to be looking for someone, as the now just 'Citizen' greeted the Company's men. To her credit the former Noble acquitted herself well. Never blanching at even the most grievous wounded, and she didn't slow down our progress by more than half an hour. As I neared her side in the hopes of seeing her off as quickly as possible, she was conversing with the overly observant guards. One saw my approach and made the Citizen aware.

"Ah. Citizen Storm Crow, I had heard reports that your friend the Daywalker was severely injured, yet I do not see her in the wagons?" the former Princess asked me as I approached. As she did so I felt the sharp tingle of a suddenly activated magic item. It gave me just enough time to realize that my first inclination of telling her the truth was a really bad idea.

"As you say Miri is a Daywalker. She fed and she regenerated the wound almost instantly. I assume that she is with the Company's lead elements keeping the Hornmen and Gnolls honest," I replied.

"Ah, I'm glad to hear that not all of my initial reports on the fight were accurate," she started, her disappointment

197

only showing ever so slightly. "Well I've slowed your progress long enough I should be catching up with my men."

With that, Citizen Adela spun on her heel and walked to her horse, mounted it and left at a fast trot with her personal guard in the same direction that her cavalry had taken.

I started to walk besides one of the wagons, until Riley flew back down onto my shoulder. "They're out of sight of the wagons and still moving towards the front," he said.

At hearing his conformation, I quickly ran towards the wagon that Miri had been in and pulled the back curtain. Sure enough, Miri was there sleeping again, though she looked to be in less pain than she had been before. Beside her was Keira changing her stomach dressings. The edges of the wounds, while close were black with corruption and smell of rot was overwhelming. Looking through the wagon I saw that all the other wounded were asleep, and thus spared the stench.

"Lucky buggers," said Riley giving voice to my thoughts.

"Get the fresh bandages out of my pack," said the book mage indicating a pack to her side. Her hands were covered by an ointment that she was spreading across the edges of Miri's wound.

Breathing through my mouth I once again stepped gingerly over the sleeping bodies to where Miri lay. Only then did I realize that the rotting smell came from what Keira was lathering onto Miri not Miri herself.

"What in the nine hells is that?" I gagged to Keira as I pulled out several fresh linen dressings.

"One of my best anti-poison poultices; we need to get Miri up and moving as quickly as possible. Her royal citizenship won't like that you lied to her about Miri's whereabouts when she finds out," she replied as she was about to wipe her hands on her dress skirt.

"Keira! No! Here," I said as I handed the book mage a bandage. I might have been worried about my lover's health, but I couldn't bear the thought of Keira subjecting all the other wounded to that smell.

Keira took the cloth wiped her hand with it and then blew her nose. After grossing me out, yet again, she said "I know Miri's wanted by the Phoenix Republic though I don't know why."

"Family," I said.

"Oh? Well since the Princess has given her lands to the undead I figured that Miri would have been part of the bargain. So, I used a simple illusion to prevent her from seeing Miri. She might be all for this bullshit about being equal before death but she's no investigator."

"True that, so now what?" I asked. When Keira was faced with a problem; that big brain of her's attacked it with as much skill as Miri used with her sword.

It was then that I noticed the wagon had sped up, and was now creaking and swaying at rate that would have drawn the driver a shift rebuke from Keira not half an hour earlier.

"We get back to camp as quickly as possible and you two get out of this Principality. Now Miri's going to be asleep for the duration of the trip. Why don't you sit up with the driver and keep a look out for trouble," she said with a surprising firmness.

Rather than arguing, I did as I was told, and moved up to sit beside the driver. As we drove through what was once familiar land I was stunned by changes that had been wrought over the land. Once again, the Phoenix Republic appeared to have been one step ahead of everyone else. The Prince hadn't even been formally buried yet, and the Republic was undoing everything that he had tried to do, as he fought to keep his people independent and free. Already the mortal inhabitants of the land were trickling back to their old villages to rebuild their homes with supplies provided free when they swore their citizenship oaths to the Republic. Their robota would be replaced by the untiring arms of the undead. Skeletons would now finish repairing the wall of the keep. In the spring zombies would be herded into the land to do manual labour in the fields. Ghouls would be freed to hunt vermin and other 'pests' on the land. In the Summer, an entire undead legion would march in as the appointed protector for this new portion of the Republic.

The people now free of their obligations to the former authorities would be allowed to prosper all equal as citizens of the New Republic. Everything logical, everything efficient, everyone equal in both opportunity and outcome. I was all for equality, and there was a lot in this world that needed fixing, but as one of my aunts was fond of saying 'to much of a good thing is a bad thing'. As I pondered all of the implications I thought back to the audience Miri and I had with the prince. Had Stain provoked Miri and I? I thought back to the Princess's reactions. Idealistic and perhaps too comfortable in her beliefs; how much of a shock had she taken from my and Miri's displays of raw power? I remember the stunned look on her face. Was that the first time that the realization that just because you were a noble didn't mean all that much when there were beings like Daywalkers and Mages that could kill you in a second? If she had than the Princess, now Citizen, Adela would have jump at the chance for the Republic's 'equality'. I wondered how much longer Citizen Adela would remain human. The Republic didn't like to have 'mere mortals' as heads of state when Vampires and Liches were supposed to be the 'natural rulers' of the nation.

But these thoughts were not my concern right now. Now I was more worried about keeping Miri out of the Republic's grasp. Fortunately, I had Keira on my side for this. An hour out from our camp we were met by a small troop of Hobgoblin scouts, with them were our horses and

Gregor's mules.

"I was able to scry a message to the quartermaster and he's got your and Gregor's animals packed as best he could without attracting notice. Your best chance is for you and Miri to head east out of this land into the Schwarzwald. No one owns that forest and I doubt they'd be willing to follow you too deep in there. Now here drink this," rambled Keira as she helped an awake but still somewhat groggy Miri out wagon and onto one of the horses.

Drinking the potion down I suddenly felt energized, more alert, and readier to face the day than I could ever remember feeling before.

"As close as I've ever been able to come to an elixir of life," explained Keira seeing the expression on my face. "I've given one to Miri as well, which is how she's able to move. Now you just feel like you can conquer the world, you don't actually have any additional reserves or power to do so.

I nodded in understanding then pulled a large sack out of my bag of holding followed by Gregor's ax cleaned and freshly oiled. I then tied both to one of the mules and handed the reins to Keira.

"Could you see that Gregor's people get these? And tell them he was good man respected by all that knew him. Tell them he died well after saving the lives of two friends," I said to her.

"I will," she said.

With that I got up on the same horse as Miri and making sure she had a tight hold of me, took the reins of the other animals and headed east into yet another unknown.

A Mortal Sacrifice

Chapter 1

Three days after we'd made our escape from Ulm, we were as close to death as we'd been when we had started out. Our mounts were exhausted and we'd needed to find a warm place to rest or all three of them would some become lame. On top of this, a second much stronger winter storm had hit, and large wet flakes of snow were falling thick, making everyone and everything cold and wet despite our magically enhanced cold weather clothing.

Miri's wounds, despite Keira's infusions were still not healing as well as they should have. Her pain was constant and she moved in and out of delirium. Despite Keira's reassurance, her infusions were not as effective on Miri as they should have been. Whether it was because of the 'cheaper' healing potions or the Titan poison I didn't know. Still I was grateful; being gutted by that Gnoll shaman's magic spear would have killed anyone else I knew of, with the possible exception of Roland. That she was still alive was enough for me. I tried to help as best I could; riding double and holding her up in the saddle, and leaving her tied on the horse when I had to blaze a trail through the woods.

Then there was my own condition. Along with the head and burns to my hands, I was trying to recover from the inevitable backlash that had resulted from nearly twenty-four hours' worth of near constant spell casting. Oh Keira's healing potions had healed all of the physical damage and had given me the energy to push hard that first day; but there had been a price. In normal circumstances I would have been asleep for a day or two recovering. But these weren't normal circumstances. I'd pushed myself so far past what I thought of as 'my limits' had been that I truly had no idea where or when my system would just say stop.

Then of course there was the Schwarzwald itself. It was a natural forest so it wasn't as thick or overgrown as the Titan Wald but it was still an old forest filled with narrow valleys, gullies and steep stream beds. It had deer trails and old roadways but it was easy to lose track of the path with the fresh snow. It didn't help that I wasn't the forester that Gregor or even Miri were and that I often had to backtrack.

One advantage of our situation was that it didn't leave me much time to ponder the thought that Gregor was actually dead. I'd lost friends before, and I'd seen a lot of other mortals die as gruesomely. But the pure senselessness of the event, the stupid way Gregor's death happened caused me to tear up far too often.

Of course, during all of this wallowing in self pity; Riley just had to be Riley. On yet another backtrack he said, "I know we're running mostly away from something Sasha, and I do think that's a good idea. Have you given any real thought as to where were running to?"

I paused for a moment and realized that my familiar had just asked me a rather profound question, given our current situation. As well I also came to the profound realization I had no absolutely no answer to that question, and said as much to Riley.

"I thought as much," he started "We've been heading deeper into the forest on a more or less eastward direction for about twenty kilometres, which given the circumstances isn't to bad. In another thirty we should hit the new Imperium Highway running between the Eisen Dwarf Holds and the Frozen Sea."

"And you think we should head south when we hit highway and see if we can find some of my kin with those Dwarves? Sounds like a plan to me," I interrupted.

"Need I remind you that's the logical answer, and that along with the Republic we're still being hunted by

Malicious and his followers who would expect you to go to ground where you would feel the safest? No, we head north get to the Frozen Sea and take an ice ship to Gothland. You, setup shop as a seamstress and make a small fortune for the next eight months using those rituals that you learned from Sariel introducing Florenz's current fashions a year before the country would normally get them," Riley said.

I hated to admit it but his plan did make a lot of sense. "Alright sounds like a plan I agreed. Now we just have to get those thirty kilometres.

Unfortunately, we never made those additional thirty kilometres. On the end of the third day all of those obstacles to our survival finally crashed in on me. Earlier that day, my body's exhaustion had caused me to lose control of my magic and I'd brought forth an intense sleet storm. I'd gotten the magic back under my control soon after, but not before everyone had been covered by a thin sheet of bone chilling ice. Lacking adequate shelter, we had to keep moving forward or risk freezing. Finally, with darkness closing in, I found a small hollow that would protect us on two sides from the wind. This had been the best campsite that I had come across that day, and I knew that it was going to be the best we could hope right now. I took care of the horses feeding them the last of the oats we'd brought, and covered them with their blankets. I then had every intention of building a fire for Miri and myself before pitching our tent, when I realized that I no longer felt cold. In fact, I was feeling quite warm. So warm in fact I took off my tricorne and scarf and opened my greatcoat.

"Sasha; what are you doing," asked Riley.

"Nothing I'm just feeling warm for the first time in four days," I said. When had first dismounted I had left Miri wrapped up in one of our bedrolls. Looking down at her now, I thought she looked so comfortable that I finished taking off my outer clothing and joined her in the bedroll.

"Sasha you need more beer," said Riley.

The last thing I remember was asking Miri if she wanted another beer because Bird Brain was buying the next round.

Chapter 2

I awoke, in the presence of a type of magic that I'd never encountered before. It felt larger than this world, similar to the Titan magic used by druids, shamans and bearshirts. Only that magic always felt and smelled wrong to me; and this magic felt somehow right. Which was a good thing; because the next thing I became aware was that this new magic was moving through me.

I must have reacted badly to the intrusion because the next thing I heard was Riley saying, "Sasha! Calm down, Alger is trying to help."

I'd admit the sound of my familiar's voice was comforting, and it was then that I decided to finally open my eyes. After blinking several times, I saw that Riley was on my chest, looking down at me his head cocked to one side as it usually did when he was concerned about something I'd done. Next to him was one of the strangest mortals I'd ever seen. He was human and looked to be in the high end of his sixties. His build was still strong however, stocky and broad shouldered; he looked like someone used to carrying great weights. His face was wrinkled and that of someone who'd walked a hard road. Yet when I looked in his eyes, and saw his smile, it was clear that he was unbowed by neither the age nor weights he'd been forced to carry. I knew that it was irrational: but I suddenly felt very safe and that this was a man who could be trusted.

"Welcome back my young friend. I'm very glad to see that you are still with us," he said; his voice as strong and as reassuring as any that I've ever heard.

"Miri?" I started to ask.

"She's fine, Alger was able to withdraw the poisons from her body and she's finally healing properly," said Riley as he pointed his beak to my right.

Looking that direction, I saw Miri in the next bed, still asleep, but looking as healthy as if she'd fed recently.

"It was a bit of a challenge to heal a Daywalker, but Aigle guided my hands true, and I was successful. You caused me far more concern. Your horses are fine as well in fact they were in much better shape than either of you when we found you," said Alger, a note of approval in his voice.

"Thank you. And please do not think that I'm ungrateful but where are we? How did we get here? And how long have we been wherever here is?" I asked.

"The building you are resting in was once a monastery dedicated to Aigle the Goddess of Light the Sun and 'The People', now occupied by the Germeide; the Community. We were guided to your location at Aigle's direction. It is a little past noon now, so you've been here for just half a day. But not to worry, Aigle still guards this place and neither the undead nor demon can find it, let alone breech its defences. You are quite safe," replied Alger.

As the words sank in I stiffened in fear. Aigle was the name of one of the Gods that broke the covenant with us mortals at the start of the Red Death. We were now being sheltered by people who were naïve enough to still believe that this God would help them in a time of their need. We were still in as great a danger as we ever were.

207

Chapter 3

If this place hadn't been a community of crazy people who were traitors to mortals everywhere, it really would have been a wonderful place to stay and heal up. The food was excellent; the beds were warm and the rooms quiet. Miri and I slept long, deep and free of nightmares: and our healing was quicker than if we'd been in Keira's care.

My first real shock with the place, were the people themselves. I hate to admit it but I had some real strong prejudice against those who worship 'Higher Beings'. In my defence, my only real reference points were the stories told by my Dwarven aunts and uncles, and the behaviour of the 'true believers' of the various Demon cults I'd encountered. Neither source had left me with a very positive perception of those who gave themselves over to 'other worldly' beings.

But the followers of Aigle were of a very different sort. First off, all of them felt very real; like they had no public mask. They were just who they were; warts and all. That level of honesty can start to creep you out after a while. They were also just so accepting, I mean even today many people (mostly those who were adults before the plague) disapprove of Miri's and mine relationship; because it's between an Elf (as most people see Miri) and a Human, or two women, or both.

But these people.

Their reactions to the fact that Miri and I were lovers were: 1. joy that we'd found someone to care about in these troubled times. 2. wanting all the gory details on how we met; and 3. the gentle but persistent suggestion that we should make our relationship official with a marriage ceremony.

Just to see how far their accepting attitudes went, I tried something. When the young woman who acted as our nurse came in I asked, "Tracy may I ask you for a favour?"

The young girl barely starting to flower into a woman replied, "of course Sasha, but I might not be able to get to it right away."

"My familiar has a particular fondness for eyeballs. Any chance you could get some for him?" I said if I just asked for another blanket.

"Eyeballs?" Tracy asked as if she'd not heard me properly.

"Yes eyeballs, cow, sheep, goat, or pig would be fine, but if you have any from wild game they would serve as well," I explained.

"I'm not sure," she paused thinking for a second; she then said, "When I'm done with my chores, I'll ask the cooks about it."

"Oh, that would be fine," I said.

"And I don't mind if they're a few days old, or cooked," added Riley speaking in front of Tracy for the first time.

"You talk?" she asked Riley, her eyes getting wider as she spoke.

"Yes, I do; and Sasha's quite correct, I really do like eyeballs. If you did get some I really would appreciate it," he said to Tracy.

"I'll keep that in mind," replied Tracy to the Raven as she turned to go about her chores.

I had thought that would be the end of the matter, until I talked to Tracy the next day. However, a few hours later Tracy returned to our room. "I talked to the cooks and while they don't have any at this time, they'll set them aside next time they butcher a pig," she said.

"Okay, thank you for letting me know," I said; looking at Riley with a mixture of surprise and annoyance. You really had to watch what you said around these people.

The other, and far greater, surprise came when I took a look at Miri's wounds. Miri and I had been moved out of the hospital and into a small guest room with a single wide

209

bed with half a dozen thick wool blankets. Getting ready for our first evening alone in the same bed for days, I had won the toss and she had to empty the chamber pot in the outhouse before turning in. So, when she returned I was already in bed, nestled under all the blankets nice and warm. While I've not had any real comparisons, I believe we're quite energetic as lovers; so, I was a little concerned about Miri's flexibility.

"Is the scar hurting when you move around?" I asked.

"What scar?" she asked a confused look on her face.

Now it was my turned to be confused, "the scar where you were eviscerated by the Gnoll's spear," I replied. Keira had to double stitch the cut to keep it close.

Instead of answering Miri just slipped off her nightshirt and showed me her naked form. Her only new blemishes were the goosebumps from just being outside.

"Riley! Get in here now!" I cried out for my familiar.

"What's wrong? Keira's infusions combined with the fact I'm a Daywalker have allowed me to heal without scars before," said Miri still confused by my reaction.

Before I gave her a response I heard several pecks at the door. Getting out of bed, I quickly went over to the door, and opened it wide enough so that Riley could hop in.

"What's going on? I thought you and Miri wanted to be alone tonight?" he asked. He sounded sleepy; I must have woken him up with my cry.

"Look!" I said frantically pointing at Miri's still naked and unscarred front.

Riley sighed and looked towards Miri, his head cocked to one side; it quickly cocked the other way in the realization as to what he wasn't seeing finally dawned upon him.

"Shit. I'd forgotten just how well Divine healing worked. Though Miri I'd get under the bedding or at least put something on your feet. Daywalker or no, it's still easy to catch a chill on these stone floors.

Suddenly I thought back to that magic that I had felt when I first awakened. How different it had felt. "That was Divine magic?" I asked Riley.

"Well yes, Alger is the leader of this group of worshipers. Why are you surprised that he can channel Divine magic?" asked Riley.

"Because I thought that you needed Gods to provide the energy to be channelled in the first place and haven't the Gods turned their backs on mortals?" I asked.

"Well he must be able to channel the magic because didn't he say that Aigle guided them to where we were and that her power protects this place?" asked Miri.

"Oh, come on, you of all people didn't recognize someone talking a good game?" I asked her.

"Well I was nearly eviscerated so I wasn't that with it then," replied Miri.

Ignoring her responses for a second, I turned my attention back to Riley. The Raven opened his beak as if to say something and then closed it again. He then cocked his head and opened his beak and then closed it again all the while not saying a word. Finally, he said "I have no idea, maybe you should ask Alger next time you see him. But right now, I'm going back to the nice warm spot near Tracy's room. They're making pretzels tomorrow morning and the lovely girl said she'd get me a fresh one."

With that the Raven hopped out of our room and flew his way down the hall.

Chapter 4

I decided to follow up on Riley's suggestion about talking to Alger the next day. All of our dirty clothing had been washed and mended including my beloved tricorne hat which I feared I was going to have to permanently replace due to the wide gashes and deep blood stains. But the Germeide had worked another miracle and both it and my greatcoat had been mended and cleaned so that while they looked new they were still broken in all the right places.

Under my signature outer clothing, I dressed in my favorite broken in blouse, pants and riding boots. As a final touch I slid Thunder and Lightning into their places along the side of the great coat. I probably didn't need them but we were still being hunted so I just felt safer with them.

Trying to find Alger was also my first chance to really get a look at the outside of the place where we had been staying for the past few days. Once again, I was impressed, despite myself, by the complex which the Germeide called home. It was setup like a small village with all the buildings surrounding a central common. The largest of these buildings was what I assumed was the church or temple. On either side of this building were dormitories where most of the followers lived. A small stable and blacksmith, a large kitchen with attached dining hall and a pottery kiln completed the buildings next to the common. Behind these buildings were a series of smaller storage buildings and of course half a dozen outhouses.

I found that I was immediately attracted to the inner buildings and it was then that I realized that they were all twice as long as they were wide; a symmetry that really appealed to the Human eye. The outer shell of all of the building's next to the common was made of the same white stone as the Old Empire roads and possessed a similar magic. So despite what I imagine was years of weathering all the buildings gleamed white and new. The same stone had been used to create a walkway around the common with a series of spokes crisscrossing the green space. All of this allowed someone to walk from any of the inner circle buildings to another without having to trudge through a foot of snow and mud.

I found the leader of the nicest group of lunatics you could meet, behind the kitchen besides the woodshed. There he and a young man were using a two person saw to buck a large pine log into fireplace size pieces. In reality Alger was actually doing the cutting, the boy was more often than not just pulling the saw back so that the older man could actually do the work.

"Ah Frauline Storm Crow. I did not expect to see you up so early. I was under the impression that it was the first night that you and your companion were spending alone.

"Why would that make them want to sleep late?" asked the boy who was at most twelve.

"Ahhh," was all that Alger could say.

"Is this one of those questions I should be asking my parents about sir?" asked the boy.

"Yes! In fact, why don't you ask them now? I'm sure the young lady can take your place," replied the older man suddenly embarrassed by the whole conversation.

The youth sulked off sure that he was, yet again, being sent away just as the conversation was getting interesting. Despite the mood that I was in I couldn't help but smile: which suddenly made me feel angrier. These were good people. This place was one of the warmest and safest places that I have been since I left the Dwarf hold. Yet it was all based on a lie. A lie that this man, who wrapped himself in the cloak of a warm caring honest man, perpetuated that lie and kept the others wrapped up in it as tight as any leader of a Demon Cult that I have ever heard of.

Seeing the rage upon my face and reading the pain under it, Alger's said "Go ahead and ask." His face so calm that it made me angrier.

"How could you side with the beings that betrayed us? That caused the deaths of so many; that left so many children without parents. Children who can't remember what their parents even looked liked, and the guilt they feel because of something that they don't have any control of," I shouted at him. I had lost enough control that I had started to channel my storm magic. My voice amplified to that of a clap of thunder. The icicles on the eaves of the kitchen broke off and fell to the ground, while the snow on the roof of the wood shed slid off. Where had the rage come from? I had not been angry when I set out to find him, just curious. Then it hit me. Here was a man that I could get some answers from: answers to questions so painful that they had lain hidden in my soul like a cyst under years of scar tissue: answers that I believe every mortal in the Mid Reich wanted answers to. I then had the very humbling feeling that I wasn't just asking these questions for myself but for every mortal.

I suddenly became afraid of being overwhelmed with that responsibility so I plunged ahead before my 'better judgement' got a hold of me.

"If you haven't noticed the world's a pretty fucked up place right now. The Titans are pushing mortals around in the wild areas, and the Demons are making life miserable in the cities. People like Miri and I. We're trying to fight the good fight, but good people are still dying for no good fucking reason, and people who should have had our back; stabbed us there, and others are helpless to stand up to them. Yet here you are sitting safe and pretty in your little corner of paradise on earth not giving a shit. Maybe that's the problem; you are the Gods in your own piece of paradise. Why should you give a shit about the rest of us? You have yours. To the hell with the rest of us," I finished. I felt so exhausted by my explosion but I also strangely felt relieved. Like that cyst had been finally lanced. I also realized that rationally I just made absolutely no sense, but

214

emotionally there was a lot of truth to it.

"What were their names?" Alger asked as I caught my breath.

"Whose names?" I asked my rant disrupted by Alger's question.

"Your parents; the ones who faces you can't remember. What were their names?

"I don't know. My first memories are of the Dwarf orphanage where I was warm, loved and cared for like I was more precious than my weight in gold," I said wiping my eyes. Somewhere in my rant I had started to cry.

"That's not your fault, not being able to remember your parents, nor being one of the lucky ones who survived so many of the years of madness in a home where you were loved, when so many grew up wretched. The Red Death has left every survivor with their own set of unique scars; often about things that we were in no control of. One of my scars is a God's frustration and shame at wanting desperately to stop the dying but being unable to," said the old man sadly.

I looked at him confused.

"The Gods, well Aigle at least, didn't abandon mortals to their fate. She tried and tried to help to stop or even slow the Red Death but there was nothing that she could do. The plague just didn't respond to any magic that she, nor any of the other Gods knew," he continued

I'd certainly never heard that before.

"You talk about being stabbed in the back? I know that pain well. The madness was kicked off by mortals turning their anger, that same anger that you just displayed, against the followers of the Gods. What few of us remained after the plague at least. So many of Aigle's clergy died in those five years trying to do what they could to help ease the suffering: turning to the mortal tools of hard work and compassion, when the God's tools failed. Soon only our largest temples could maintain even a skeleton staff of clergy and lay members.

And then the demagogues started. The people were hurt, and angry; they were looking for someone to blame. The Red Death had to be someone's fault and the demagogues pointed towards the Gods and their earthly servants and said 'There! There are the villains! The Gods could have cured us of the plague as they cured us of every other illness before it. They chose not to this time. They've turned their backs on you. Let us punish those who stayed safe against plague,"

I looked at Alger's face and saw the sadness on it. It was a pain that I had no idea of how deep it ran. Old wounds were opening for both of us in this 'fight'.

"Suddenly, as if by magic, everything that Aigle had done for the people was forgotten. We were now mortal's great enemies. It was the one and only time that my sword tasted innocent blood and I defended my brothers and sisters from the mob; giving them time to run. Aigle was still able to power many of my abilities then and I used them to cow the mob in a desperate attempt to reduce the number of deaths all around. But that just backfired. I enraged the mob even more by showing that I truly still possessed Aigle's gifts and was using them to try and keep them in line.

"Then finally on one horrible day Aigle's powers stopped working. Her followers were too few now for her to channel the magic to us anymore. She apologized for her failures and begged us to do whatever we needed to survive.

"For the first time in ten years I was truly alone. It was then that the blackness entered my soul. I was desperate enough to rejoin Aigle that I thought seriously about ending my own life. Yes such despair was a sin, but I was sure Aigle would have forgiven me. I know several clerics of Aigle, and the other Deities as well, that actually did end their own lives to join their Gods. But in the end I decided that just because Aigle couldn't help me that didn't mean I couldn't help Aigle. I knew of this monastery and started to bring the survivors of the laity to it from around the Northern Imperium. Here we'd keep the flame of what Aigle was and what we who served her did, alive. One day the world will be ready to hear her teachings again and when it is we will be here.

"While I was here, I also learned that I could channel my own life force to power some of the simpler gifts that Aigle provided like basic healing and enriching the soil so we could grow enough crops to keep us going," the big man explained.

Everything that he said left me a bit stunned. Mortals had turned on the Gods? We were the ones who broke the Compact? This completely opposed what everyone took as the hard truth for years: and yet. And yet what Alger said had what one of my uncles would say was the ring of truth. Certainly it did not seem implausible during the Years of Madness. But something else that he had said caught my attention. Channel his life force?

Suddenly something clicked in my head and I asked "Just how old are you?"

"I turned forty-two this year; an auspicious year for some. But for me; just another year. And please don't tell me how old I look. When I was your age I was horrible at telling others age," replied Alger.

And there it was why Alger appearance seemed so strange to me. He aged every time he used the magic that originally a God had powered for him.

"The healing you did on Miri and me: how much did that shorten your life?" I asked.

"Just a few weeks, a month at most: a small price to pay to give you both decades more of life. Who knows what you will be able to do with those decades. How many people you will be able to save. How many wrongs you will be able to make right," he said.

217

I felt very humble right then, and ashamed that I had just shouted at him before. This man had sacrificed his own existence on the idea that Miri and I could do more with our time then he could with his.

"You gambled a lot on two perfect strangers," I said not really even sure I wanted to accept the mantle that he was giving me.

Alger smiled "Not really, your friend advocated very hard on both of your behalves. Tell me does Riley just prefer the bird form or is he cursed? I only ask because I believe that we have a remove curse scroll in the library. It's been there for years. We'd not miss it if it put a good man back into his original body"

"Riley? No he's not a mortal; he's my familiar. That is his original form," I replied surprised. Given what I assumed was years of experience I would have thought he'd run into at least one other familiar.

"I've met many familiars in my time, attached to many different mages. None of them have been anywhere near as independent or as capable as Riley. Where did you find the ritual to summon him?" he asked genuinely curious.

"I didn't summon him. After the lightning strike that made me into a wild mage I was in a lot of pain and unable to control my new powers. On one particularly rough night I accidentally burnt one of my favorite childhood stuffed animals; a raven I had called Riley. The smoke had blown out of my room through the window. When I turned to look at the window tears in my eyes I saw a real Raven sitting there. He said that his name was Riley and that he was my familiar and that he'd help me gain control of my new powers," I said smiling remembering that night.

"Then he's like no familiar that I've known. But surely other mages must have talked to you about this?" he asked.

I thought of Keira and couldn't believe that the book mage could have missed something like that. Then I suddenly thought of the strange way she always acted

218

around Riley. How formal they were with each other. Was her strange behavior more than just a fear of birds?

"I'm sorry I've clearly upset you and that wasn't my intent," said Alger seeing the expression upon my face. "He's not malicious in any, way I would have known that. And he genuinely cares for both of you deeply.

He then pointed towards one of the side buildings and said, "Our library has a few magical texts. Please feel free to see what they say about familiars before you talk to him further. I'm not an expert on wild magic and maybe that's how some wild mages gain their companions."

Chapter 5

We spent the next two weeks at the Monastery healing both physically and emotionally. At first, we continued to sleep a lot, eat too much food and generally didn't do much at all. This lasted three days before both of us were crawling out of our skin with inactivity. Fortunately, the monastery's community had a lot of suggestions as to how we could help. We were immediately put upon the chore list and soon we were both elbows deep in washing dishes, maintaining buildings and taking care of the monastery's small herds of sheep and cattle. Actually, it wasn't as hard as it could have been. Both of us still had plenty of time in the day for other activities.

The church had long ago been turned into a sheltered community meeting place, which included an Old Empire style gymnasium where Alger encouraged people to exercise during the winter so that they wouldn't get too 'settled' during the slower months. Miri spent several hours there each day exercising and in weapon's training. Needless to say, she attracted a lot of attention from the younger members of the Germeide. So, Miri being Miri started 'self-defence' classes and trained the laity in weapon and foot work. Fortunately, she was smart enough to take my advice and talked to Alger first. He was happy about Miri's offer but did suggest that she kept weapon's training limited to the quarterstaff.

I ended up helping out the two seamstresses of the group; mostly by showing them how to cast Sariel's clothing rituals. While they preferred to sow the clothing by hand, they did like how they could change their basic wool and linen cloth into not only other materials, but also other colours. Soon everyone had colourful silk head scarfs and handkerchiefs with colourful dresses promised soon. I got a blue fine wool neck scarf as a thank you; that I treasured for the rest of that winter.

I also followed up with Alger suggestion and consulted the Germeide library's regarding familiars. I had to be careful when I did this, the last thing I wanted was Riley to know what I was doing. But he had gained a following from the children of the community who thought that a talking Raven was the most wonderful thing ever. Suddenly the Germeide had a new story teller who was more than happy to regale an audience for hours at a time. It felt strange keeping secrets from my oldest and dearest friend. Miri and I were lovers which I kept in a different category than friend, but I wanted to have an idea of what I was actually dealing with before, or even if, I confronted him.

They didn't have a lot on familiars but they did have some basic magic texts whose author's names even I recognized. In regards to familiars they were all very clear; a familiar was created by the mage as both an aide to channel magic and as an assistant in academic research. They were also unanimous in saying that while the familiar was far more intelligent than their animal counterpart and that some of them could speak; they were unable to carry on a normal conversation with others. Nor did they require food, sleep or the other basic functions of a living creature.

So, by their definition Riley wasn't a familiar. But I took heart that all of these books were written prior to the Plague hitting the Mid-Reich. So much had changed in the world since then; who could say how familiars were created now. And it wasn't as if wild mages hadn't shown unusual abilities when it came to magic, my fight with the druid had shown that. Should I let matters lie? I mean aren't we all entitled to our secrets?

Later that night after a quiet bout of love making, I told Miri everything I had found out and asked her opinion.

Her response was simple and so Miri, "Let the Bird Brain have his secrets. He's a friend and a companion, but I don't own him and frankly neither do you. I mean think about it. How long would we last if either of us looked as close to our motivations as you were with Riley?"

She had a point. Which actually brought up another question that I'd been meaning to ask Miri: and now seemed to be a good time. "Who have you fed upon?"

"Pardon?" asked Miri surprised.

"Who have you fed upon? You've been chipper and positive for days now and it's been over two weeks since you have fed," I said.

My lover looked at me with a surprised look upon her face. "It has been that long hasn't it. Sasha to tell the truth I've not fed on anyone because I've not felt the hunger," she said with surprise in her voice.

"What!" now I was surprised.

"It's true until you mentioned it I've honestly not thought about it. Maybe it is this place or these people. I'd never felt as welcome as I do here, nor as safe. I know we'd talked about spending the winter here but I'd been thinking that there are worst places to actually live. And if living here actually meant that I no longer had to feed on people, well that makes me want to consider that even more," she said with a hopeful seriousness that I'd never seen her have before.

"We probably have to get married," I said trying to lighten the mood.

"Would that be so bad? I mean seriously other than officially stating it publicly how aren't we married?" she countered as serious as before.

Suddenly I had a lot more to worry about than what Riley was. I panicked; uncomfortable with where this conversation was heading.

"You're right we should talk about this, but not right now," I said before I muted her reply by pressing my lips to hers. I slowly moved down her body kissing her naked flesh as I went, until finally I found her other pair of lips. There I got lucky and I was able to give Miri something to think about that was far more immediate then the idea of us getting married.

Chapter 6

The next day I spent deep in the library pretending to research something while I wrestled with my previous night's conversation with Miri. Not the least of which was the very simple question: why had Miri's suggestion of marriage disturbed me so much?

"What'cha working on?" asked Riley as he landed upon my shoulder.

I don't think he was expecting my shriek of surprise because he hopped down onto the desk and asked "What's got you so jumpy?"

"Sorry I've just got a lot on my mind," I replied.

"Oh, like what?" he asked.

"Oh, like Miri wants to get married, and wants to live here and she's not felt any desire to feed since we've been here and I want the mood swinging blood drinking Daywalker I fell in love with back before this other Miri traps me here forever," I said in one wall of sound.

"OOOkay," he said taking it all in. "Have you tried these people's schnapps? I think you could use a shot for medicinal reasons."

Riley had said dumber things in the past, but I knew myself well enough to know that one shot of schnapps would become two shots and two shots would end up being two bottles. And while getting, puke your guts out drunk, had a certain appeal to me right about then the more Dwarven parts of my nature thought that was a bad idea: for now.

Seeing that I didn't even smile at his suggestion, Riley tried a new tact, "So you're feeling a little trapped? Oh, and by the way Miri not having to feed is ultimately a good thing and I shouldn't have to be the one to tell you that."

"Don't you think I know that? Of course, Miri not wanting to feed on people is a good thing. That's why I feel so guilty about wanting things the way they were before," I said angrily. What was it about this place that gets me riled up so quickly?

"Okay Sasha I need you to take a deep breath or we're going to have a rainstorm right in the middle of these nice people's library of rare and valuable books," Riley cautioned.

Looking up I saw grey clouds had started to form under the library's ceiling. I gulped and sitting upright in my chair, with my hands at my side I started to do a basic breathing exercise that Riley had taught me years ago. By breathing slowly and deeply I calmed my mind and got control of my then turbulent emotions.

Of course, it was just as I was finally calming down, that I was nearly overwhelming wave of nausea hit me. I vomited into my mouth but kept it from going past my lips. Swallowing the bile back down I realized that someone nearby had just cast a powerful spell with Demonic magic.

I looked with horror towards Riley and said "Demons!"

He just nodded and pointed towards where I had hung my great coat and hat. Without a further word, I moved towards my battle gear and opening my bag of holding withdrew the belt on which Thunder and Lightning hung.

"Warn everyone, I'll find Miri and we'll see what we're dealing with," I said as I wrapped my armoured coat around me.

"Don't you dare start anything until I'm with you this time! That wasn't just a minor Demon emerging: that was something else," said Riley as he flew through the door that I had just kicked open for him.

Chapter 7

Unfortunately, the wave of Demonic magic that I felt was accompanied by a similar sized real-world manifestation. The clouds above the Germeide had turned black, completely blocking the light of the winter sun from the village. Blood red lightning flashed between the clouds turning the ground into a nightmare of black and red patches.

"What's going on?" said Miri as she suddenly flashed beside me. Her Daywalker powers appeared not to have been affected by her lack of feeding. She'd found me and was already dressed in her own patched up greatcoat her magic longsword already in hand.

"A Demon," I said as we headed towards the source of the magical energies: and stopped in my tracks as I saw that it wasn't a Demon but Demons: tens of Demons.

All but one of the Demons present were smaller creatures; about the size of human. Each one a perfectly crafted horror. The one larger Demon was roughly the same size as the Minotaur we fought just a few weeks ago. However, this creature appeared to be largely human with only his black horn and red skin betraying his other worldly origins.

"Ah Storm Crow; I knew my calling would bring you out of the hole you were hiding in," said the large Demon.

I knew that voice. Despite it being a different tone, (not to mention volume) its cadence was unforgettable.

"Malicious," I said with as much venom as I could muster. The nearby loose snow started to move; swirling into a mini snowstorm around me as the magic responded to my emotional state.

"In the flesh. You've led me on a merry chase little girl. But ultimately a far more rewarding one than I originally expected. Here you are in the last bastion of a lost God. With both of you and this place destroyed, not only will I have corrected a mistake, but weakend one of my greatest foes enough that I many possess one of the greatest prizes in the Reichs," the Demon said cackling all the way.

"This idiot does love the sound of his own voice, doesn't he?" said Riley as he landed on my shoulder.

"Ah the exile, I was wondering where you were. Tell me coward how do you justify your existence when your brethren sacrificed themselves to start all of this off?"

"Wouldn't you like to know?" said Riley his tone flat.

What was that all about? I thought to myself; but now was not the time wonder about those kinds of issues. Riley was right, Malicious was a talker, and a talker liked to drag the start of the battle out so that he could attack his opponent's confidence.

I wasn't going to allow Malicious that luxury.

I had drawn my foci when I saw the Demons and I now to started to consciously draw upon the magic to power my spells.

"Sasha no! The Demon wants you to attack him, and his brethren. Look at how they're deployed. The barrier that Aigle created when the monastery was first built still protects this place against immortal evil. Malicious and his minions cannot enter here.

"So, we're safe if we don't attack?" asked Miri.

I heard foot steps behind us and was horrified to see ten or so of Miri's 'students' running up to where we were; unarmoured and carrying the quarterstaffs that they had only recently started to train with. Behind them were another twenty or so villagers armed and armoured with a variety of weapons, all of which were clearly old but well maintained.

"What are they doing here?" I hissed to Miri.

"They want to defend their home Sasha, not hide while others fight their battles for them," replied Miri with a note of approval in her voice.

"I see the gangs all here, and since the exile has spoiled my plan A I guess I have to start with plan B," said Malicious as he grabbed up one of his Demon minions and flung it toward me.

With a sickening thud the smaller Demon splatted across an invisible barrier between Malicious and where Miri and I stood. Its body burst on impact, sending black Demon blood and guts sideways out across the barrier.

"This is why I brought so many friends," said the large Demon as he grabbed a second minion and flung it as well. This was followed by a third.

Behind us I heard more than one person wretch at the sight.

"Riley am I right in guessing that he's using the smaller Demons blood and life force to weaken the spiritually opposite barrier," I asked the Raven.

"If this were any other situation I'd be really proud of your growth in the understanding of the arcane Sasha. But right now, all I have is that you are absolutely correct, and there is nothing we can do to stop him," replied Riley his voice strained in fear.

For perhaps the first time on an arcane issue Riley was wrong. There was something I could do. I was sure a wild magical spell like the one I'd used to kill the Druid several months before would also end Malicious. I'd survived that last spell more by luck than anything else, and that kind of luck doesn't come twice in a year. But there was no way that I was going to allow these good (though still insane) people to die because they had made the mistake of helping me and Miri.

With a deep breath I turned to Miri whose grim resolve was evident not only on her face but her body as well. She wasn't going to back down either. I grabbed her by the back of the head and turned her to face me as I kissed her hard one last time.

"I love you. Never forget that. Do what you have to, to defend everyone else. You're all that's going to stand between them and damnation," I said, surprised at how calm I sounded.

Miri's eyes widened in understanding but at the sound of another Demon being killed against the barrier she just nodded and then turning towards the villagers she said "Everyone get back! Sasha is going to kill that big ass demon and you definitely do not want to be caught in the backlash.

"You get going to Riley. Miri's going to need your help, here as well," I said to my familiar as I refocused my attention on Malicious.

The soft rubbing of his feathers against my cheek broke my will at last and I started to tear up.

"If you think I'm going to let you try and control raw magic alone again Sasha you are sadly mistaken. Now think of a wide area blasting forward, not just a straight line. You're going to have to take out a fair number of the little shits along with Malicious to give everyone else a chance," Riley said with a determined voice.

With a nod to my familiar, I straightened, adjusted the Tricorne and started to once again open myself fully to the magic around me.

And nothing happened.

It is a very strange feeling to start something that you know will kill you and have it stopped before you actually die.

I angrily turned to Riley thinking he'd done something, but he appeared as surprised to still be alive as I was.

"I didn't heal your body and take on the venting of your soul just for you to kill yourself a few weeks later young lady," said Alger as he placed his hand upon my shoulder. "Now is not your time."

I turned and saw the old Sun worshiper standing next

to me. He was dressed in a suit of full steel plate armour that was old even before the Red Death. On his left arm was a kite shield of thick wood covered in leather. In his right hand was a silver steel sword a metre and half in length. Alger glowed in magic with a light so bright that it was hard to actually look at him. How I'd missed his approach was beyond me. I guess he had somehow cloaked his divine magic from everyone.

"Take care of everyone Sasha, and if you both survive you really should allow Miri to make an honest woman of you," he said to me as he lowered his helmet's visor and started calmly walking towards Malicious.

When he saw Alger approaching Malicious stopped mid throw to gawk at the armoured mortal.

"A paladin? I thought we killed the last of the Sun Knights years ago? Well this is turning into a great day indeed," he said as he flung another Demon this time aimed at Alger.

There was a shattering sound as this Demon went through the barrier and continued towards Alger. Seeing the incoming flesh missile Alger braced his legs and raised the shield. The Demon impacted upon the wood barrier and splattered across it like its brothers had splattered across Ailger's barrier. Impossibly Alger was still standing, not only that but when he started to move towards the large Demon again he started to run. His steel shod legs actually propelling him across the top of the snow without sinking.

Suddenly the Demons weren't as confident. Many of the smaller ones started to back away, while Malicious appeared to panic. Grabbing two of the smaller Demons at a time he started to hurl them at Alger without taking the time to aim. Alger dodged three of the Demons and cut the forth completely in half with a single swipe of his long sword.

Then it was Alger's turn to strike. With a cry, that was clear even through his closed helm, the old Sun Knight leapt three metres into the air his sword becoming incandescent as he flew. We were all blinded by the flash as the sword hit Malicious square in the chest. The Demon's death scream deafened all the mortals as the blow ended his existence forever.

To say that Alger channeled divine magic into that attack was obvious. But the amount was staggering. I just knew that no one could expend that much life energy and live. Alger had sacrificed himself so that everyone else would live. I felt a sudden flash of anger that the old man had robbed me of that moment. I was going to be the one who killed themselves to save everyone damn it! Fortunately my sanity quickly returned and the realization that I was still alive and the relief of that feeling took hold.

That feeling of relief however was quickly replaced with stunned disbelief as my vision returned and I saw Alger standing above the ashes that was all that remained of Malicious. Around him were tens of demon bodies; all burned by his divine fire. Only three Demons were left alive on the very fringes of the swarm.

"How in the name of the Three Reichs is he still alive?" I asked the space where I thought Riley was in. Only I was wrong. The Raven had flown from my shoulder and landed in front of the remaining Demons.

"You idiots! You stupid bastards! When are you fools going to get it through your thick heads that the fundamental spark that created mortals was sacrifice? That every mortal has the capacity to put the welfare of others before their own welfare," he shouted at the Demons in a voice far louder than any Raven had a right to have.

"Go and spread the word to every Demon, Titan, Old One and whatever other names my former family use because they're afraid. Tell them that Malicious has caused their plans to backfire. Because of one mortal's sacrifice a new Covenant has been forged. That they're plans around the Red Death failed and mortals will lock them into their

231

reality. Tell them one of my favorite sayings I've learned from the mortals: payback's a bitch.

With that the three Demons just disappeared as if they had never been there.

With a bouncing nod, Riley took flight once again only to land again this time in front of Alger.

"All hail Alger God of the Sun and Light, Protector and Empowerer of the Common People. I greet the first God of the New Covenant," he said again in a voice far too large and too strong for the Raven that I had known for years.

By this time Miri and I along with the rest of the inhabitants of the monastery had moved to surround their leader. As Alger took off his helm we all stopped not sure of exactly what we were seeing. Alger was still there but at the same time he wasn't. Gone were the wrinkles and silver hair; replaced by the perfectly symmetrical strong features of a man in the flower of youth. His hair a cascade of long curls the colour of the noon day sun. His eyes had been replaced with golden orbs of fire that bore into you with a gaze that left your soul open. Yet it was also clear that there was room for compassion, for laughter, for hope in that face as well.

"What happened? How am I still alive?"

"And why are your eyes glowing?" asked Miri.

Surprised at her question Alger looked at his reflection on the back of his silvered helm. "Sweet Aigle what's happening?"

"You're right it was Aigle. She always did have a soft spot for her male Paladins. Oh, she loved all of her clergy both men and women, but she had grown up on stories of heroes in shining armour saving damsels in distress and that never really left her; despite her best efforts not to let that bias her choices," explained Riley.

"I still don't understand?" said Alger.

Riley sighed and tried again, "Alger you were her last

paladin, her last Sun Knight. You were about to sacrifice yourself to save everyone else. Aigle couldn't standby; yet again, and lose someone that she loved. So, like so many parents and lovers before her, she sacrificed herself to keep you alive. The life force that was used to smite Malicious was hers. She gave up the mortal soul, that combined with the Divine Spark, made her a God."

"Why? Why did she do that? It was my duty to die in her service not for her to die in mine!" Alger wailed in despair.

I couldn't help it, in frustration I cuffed Alger hard upside the head and said, "Because she loved you, you idiot and it was the only way to keep you alive! The same reason why you stopped me from killing myself while trying to channel the raw magic."

It was only then that I realized what I had just done. I just hit a God and called him an idiot. Everyone looked at me with a 'I can't believe she just did that' expression on their faces.

"Actually, that wasn't me but Aigle as well, she was tired of watching good people sacrificing themselves to protect others from the Demons," said Alger, he then turned to Riley and asked, "How do I know that?"

Riley sighed in the same way he had done when I had been starting to first control my magic, "Okay from the top. When she died, the Divine Spark passed to the most deserving person: which was you. Alger you are now the God of the Sun and Light," he said as bluntly as possible.

"And before you say that 'you don't want to be a God' know that was Aigle's reaction as well. None of the Gods that are worth more than a bucket of piss wanted the spark. But when they got the power they did what so many mortals do in these situations; they stepped up," said Riley as he saw Alger start to open his mouth.

Riley's explanation appeared to have been enough for the Germeide. All of them knelt before their old leader and new God in homage.

That left only Alger, Miri and I standing, and while Alger was still trying to get to grips with his new status, both Miri and I were looking hard at the creature I had once thought of as my familiar.

He looked up at the both of us and coughed once, suddenly uncomfortable in our gaze.

"I guess an explanation is in order," he said finally.

Thank you for reading my book. If you liked my stories, please go back to the retailer from whom you downloaded this book and leave a short review and rating. It's feedback like that that will help me become a better writer.

About the Author

Sandy Addison has always been a story teller; either in the real-world or at the role-playing table. However, it has been only the past few years that he's gained the courage to actually share his stories with others. He has written several adult themed novellas and two short novels under a pen name, but *Sellswords* is the first fiction piece that he has published under his own name.

Connect with Sandy Addison

Favorite my Smashwords author page:
https://www.smashwords.com/profile/view/Sandy42

Made in the USA
Lexington, KY
12 April 2018